THE RECEIVER

THE RECEIVER

by

TEX MAULE

DAVID McKAY COMPANY, INC.

New York

THE RECEIVER

LIBRARY OF CONGRESS CATALOG CARD NUMBER: 68-29631

MANUFACTURED IN THE UNITED STATES OF AMERICA

For my sons

THE RECEIVER

Chapter 1

Sᴘɪᴅᴇʀ Lᴇɢɢᴇᴛᴛ made his cut and accelerated sharply. He slanted toward the corner of the end zone and the defensive halfback, unable to react with him, trailed by three steps as Spider glanced back quickly. The ball should be in the air by now, and he knew that he would have a touchdown if Brad Thomas was on target with the pass.

The defensive man turned sharply away and sped toward the other side of the field and Spider followed after him. The ball had been thrown short to Slats Shrake, the big Ram tight end and Shrake was cutting toward Leggett, bulling his way through a tackle. When the defensive back cut back to reach Shrake, Spider cut him down with a knee-high, blind side block.

The play had gained nine yards and a first down. Dick Gangel, the Rams' tall, lean flanker, slapped Spider on the back as he got to his feet.

"Way to block, Spider," he said.

"Thanks," Leggett said. He could not help a note of bitterness. He had been the intended receiver on the play, and he had beaten his man cleanly but again, Thomas, the All-Pro quarterback of the Rams, had gone to another receiver.

He stifled his resentment and ranged alongside Thomas as the players went into their huddle.

"I can beat Fox on a deep out, Brad," he said. "He was dead on that one."

Thomas looked at him noncommittally and nodded.

"I'll remember that," he said. "Good block."

Spider did not answer him. He knelt in the huddle and heard Thomas call a running play and trotted out to the left to his post as spread end. He faked a pass pattern, momentarily freezing the corner back assigned to cover him and then sprinted downfield to block on the safety should Rabbit Laguerre, the Rams' brilliant rookie halfback, break into the clear. Laguerre, a short, wide back with exceptional speed and almost indestructible balance, was buried after a short gain.

It was late in the fourth period and the Rams held a comfortable lead over the Atlanta Falcons, so Spider was not surprised when Billy Gallagher trotted onto the field and nodded at him. He unsnapped his chin strap as he made his way to the sideline, where he turned to watch the next play. Thomas had called the same deep corner pattern on which Spider had faked the Falcon defender, but this time the de-

2

fensive back stayed with Gallagher, and Brad, unable to find a free receiver, was trapped for a six-yard loss.

Frog Howard, the number two Ram quarterback, listened momentarily to last minute instructions from Head Coach Joe Steadman, then went in to replace Thomas as Steadman began clearing the bench.

Spider walked slowly to the bench and sat down next to Bob Ottum, the big running back. Ottum grinned at him.

"Halfway home, Spider," he said. "Seven down and seven to go, baby."

"Hope we can keep rolling," Leggett said. "We go six and 1 for the last half, and we'll be home free."

Ottum rapped the bench with his knuckles.

"Don't give us a jinx," he said. "It'll be tougher in the next seven games, Spider. Let's hope no one gets racked up."

The game ended a few minutes later, and Spider walked silently across the field to the tunnel leading to the dressing rooms in the Los Angeles Coliseum. He had caught three passes during the game, and Brad had thrown to him four times, although he knew he had been open often. It was part of a pattern which had developed partly during the exhibition season and partly because of the first game the Rams had played in the regular season.

The passes he had caught in this game had been short, sideline balls, and twice he had had to circle back when Thomas was scrambling, and the called patterns had been broken. Once he had dropped the ball as he was hit hard reaching for a tall pass and he remembered the dropped ball unhappily. It would not make Brad anxious to throw to him in the next game.

By now he was in the small dressing cubicle he shared

3

with Dick Gangel, the flanker who played at the opposite end of the Ram line. Gangel, a six-foot, four-inch rookie who had broken into the starting lineup when Hooks Terry, the regular Ram flanker, had separated a shoulder in the last game of the exhibition season, was still struggling to learn his patterns and the changes dictated by zone or man-to-man defenses.

He was sitting on the stool in front of his locker cutting the tape from his ankles with the special tool used for that purpose and he glanced up as Spider flopped on his own stool.

"Hey," he said. "I'm pooped. Seemed like all I ran out there today was deep patterns. And I blew some of them."

"You're doing real well," Spider said.

"I'm still having trouble reading the coverage," Gangel said. "So I zig when I should zag."

"It'll come," Spider said. He was in his third season, his first as a regular, and the patterns came to him easily now. He was beginning to feel the game, and he knew that he was playing well. If only Brad would throw to him, he thought. He looked at his hands and clenched them.

"You gonna undress?" Gangel asked.

Spider nodded and unlaced his shoes. Gangel handed him the razor, and he sliced through the tape on his ankles and ripped it off.

Gangel had stripped by now and threw a towel over his shoulder, preparing to take a shower, and Spider watched him leave the small room. As always, he felt a faint tinge of envy when he looked at Gangel. The rookie was tall, but he was powerfully built and carried 220 pounds on his long frame. Spider, who was only six feet tall, weighed a meager 172; if he hadn't had 9.4 speed in the hundred-yard dash, he

4

could never have survived. When he had come to the Rams, he had barely lasted through the final cut.

He finished taking his uniform off and cut the gauze bandages off his wrists last. He wore the gauze on his wrists to keep sweat from his arms from running down onto his hands and making them slippery. The day had been warm on the floor of the Coliseum, and the gauze was damp.

He stayed in the shower for a long time, letting the warm water ease the faint ache in his muscles and relax him. As the water poured over him, he thought back to the disastrous first game of the regular season.

He had started slowly during the exhibition games, working on smoothing his patterns and running them precisely. For the first time, he was sure that he would be the Rams' starting spread end, and he was not worried about making the club. Jim Lyman, a veteran of twelve years in the league, had retired, and Spider felt sure that he was ready for the starting job.

Thomas threw to him often in the early games, and he dropped a few balls, but he did not fret about it. It always took him a while to reach the delicate balance between controlled speed and balance which allowed him to concentrate on catching the ball, and he was sure that by the time the Rams entered the regular season, he would have no trouble.

The Rams opened the season at home against the Baltimore Colts, and Spider grimaced when he remembered with what anticipation he had faced that game. The Colts had a strong pass defense, with veteran backs and a strong set of linebackers, but their pass rush had dropped off, and Spider knew that if he had time to work, he would get free. If he were free, Brad would hit him.

5

The first call of the game was a long post pattern to him, designed to catch the Colts cold. The Rams had received and Laguerre, running back his first kickoff in regular game play, had missed by a step going all the way. When the Rams took the field, they had the ball on their own 33-yard line, in good position for the daring long pass call.

The Rams came out in a double wing set designed to force the Colt defense into single coverage on the receivers. The formation left Thomas vulnerable to a blitzing defense if the Colts wanted to commit one or more linebackers to the pass rush, but Brad knew, as well as Spider, that the Colts did not blitz much, and it seemed very unlikely that they would gamble on the first play of the game.

The formation isolated Spider on Kim Jones, the left corner back for the Colts. Jones was small for a corner back, but he had good speed, and he was a strong and punishing tackler. As Spider started downfield, he felt sure that he could get the necessary step on the other man. Jones had played him tight, and he knew that he had much better straight away speed than the defender.

He ran straight at Jones until the back gave ground, then took a quick step to the outside and looked back as if expecting the ball. Without breaking stride or looking at Jones again, he cut back sharply at a forty-five degree angle toward the center of the field, running on a heading for the goalpost.

As he finished the cut, he accelerated sharply, and he knew that he had beaten Jones. When he looked back and up over his left shoulder, the ball hung at the top of its trajectory, just nosing over, and Spider knew that it would be an easy catch. He held his speed and kept his hands down and pumping until the last moment, when he reached and stretched for the ball; it was easily in his grasp.

Just as it was settling in his hands, he glanced away, looking for the safety and dropped the ball. The safety was coming across hard and desperately, and when Spider slowed up instinctively as he felt the ball go, it allowed the defender to reach him, and he was hit hard.

The tackle did not hurt, but he was furious as he trotted back to the huddle. He had made an inexcusable mistake for a veteran receiver in taking his eyes off the ball before he had it safely in his hands, and he shook his head in disgust at himself.

Thomas glanced at him curiously as he took his place in the circle of players.

"Too far?" he asked.

"No," Spider said. It was a temptation to say the pass had been overthrown, but he did not consider using any excuse. "I looked away."

"You were open," Thomas said. "Let's try it again. They won't be looking for the same play twice in a row."

Spider nodded and when he took his three point stance on the left flank of the Ram offensive set, he gritted his teeth in determination. Again Jones took a close position on him, probably expecting now that Thomas would go for a short sideline pattern looking for the first down.

Spider gave him the same fake to the outside, but this time Jones stayed on top of him and hit him hard as he made the fake, forcing him off balance, momentarily. He fought to regain control, then cut back toward the post and ran hard, knowing that he had been slowed in the pattern. When he looked back for the ball, he knew that it was too high and too

7

far, but he sprinted desperately trying to reach it. He jumped and felt the ball tick his fingertips just as the safety hit him again, spinning him in almost a complete flip. He hit on the back of his neck and his shoulders and felt the jar with his whole body, but he jumped up again quickly. He had not seen or heard the safety coming in his concentration on the ball, and he did not feel bad as he returned to the huddle. He could not have done any better on this attempt for the completion.

"They doubling you?" Thomas asked. "That's twice the safety got to you."

"No," Spider told him. "He's got good recovery. He's dropping off to help after the ball's in the air. I just got chucked hard then when I made the first cut."

Thomas called a quick pass over the center to Shrake, the tight end, anticipating a blitz on third and long yardage, and Slats took the ball eight yards with a linebacker hanging on him. It was not far enough for the first down, and the Rams had to punt.

During the rest of that, for Spider, long afternoon, Thomas threw to him four times, and he caught two balls. Once Brad threw quickly to avoid a rush, and the ball reached Spider just as he turned and bounced off his pads.

Another pass simply slipped through Spider's hands when Jones hit him as the ball reached him. The two balls he caught were on quick turnouts at the sidelines, late in the half, when the Rams were driving for a score against the clock. The Rams had won the game, 17-14, but the strength of their attack had been in their powerful running game and in outlet passes to the running backs or short shots to Shrake, the tight end.

The game had been bad, but the Tuesday morning film session had been worse. Watching himself on the screen, Spider had cringed inwardly when he saw the ball skid out of his hands on the first long pass and off his fingertips on the second. Both times, the impact of the safety's tackle seemed much more shattering on the screen than it had been on the field.

Dickey, the Ram end coach, talked to him quietly for a little while after the meeting, reminding him to look the ball into his hands on each pass and not to run with it until he had put it in the bank. In the bank, of course, meant tucked firmly away under his arm with the tip wrapped up in the palm of his hand.

"I know, Red," Spider had told him. "I don't know what happened to me on that first one. I guess I was just keyed up with the first game of the season and all."

He had made a mental vow to watch every ball into his hands for the rest of the year, but the second game had been worse than the first. Concentrating fiercely on looking the ball home, he had tensed up, and his hands, instead of being soft and going with the ball, had felt like claws. Thomas had thrown to him four or five times, then gone to his other receivers when he found that Spider was not holding the ball.

After that second game, Thomas had thrown to Spider just often enough so that the defenses could not ignore him. During the first game and most of the second, the defenders had occasionally doubled up on Spider, but after the third, the single coverage on him had become automatic. It gave him the opportunity to get open often, but that did him little or no good, since Thomas threw to Shrake, or Gangel, or to one of the running backs.

9

Spider had had to fight himself to keep from growing bitter and to keep from asking Thomas to throw to him more. He forced himself to keep quiet and go about his business, working hard on the patterns and developing moves as he learned the habits of the defensive backs more thoroughly. He knew, by mid season, that he had become a much better receiver.

"You gonna shower all night?" Gangel brought him out of his reverie, and he realized that he was still under the spray. By now the dressing room was quiet. Most of the players had left, and only the equipment men were still at work, gathering up the dirty uniforms to send to the laundry.

Spider toweled himself hurriedly and dressed quickly. Gangel waited for him and walked with him up the long tunnel to the team parking lot just outside the Coliseum. Spider and Gangel roomed together on the road, but the big rookie was married and had a small apartment in Long Beach, near the Ram practice field. Spider lived alone in an efficiency apartment not far away, and the two players often went to practice together, leaving Gangel's car for his wife to use.

Gangel had waited for Spider because Ruth, his wife, had gone home ahead of him, anxious to get back to their 3-month-old son. He climbed into Spider's sports car and sighed.

"Rough, man," he said. "Rough. I never knew it could get so complicated."

"It gets tougher," Spider said as he drove out to Santa Barbara Street and headed for the freeway toward Long Beach. "The defensive backs learn your moves and what you can do and what you can't. This is your first season in the league, Dick. They didn't have a book on you at first, but they have one now."

10

"Thanks," Gangel said. "You really know how to make a guy feel good, Spider."

Spider glanced at him and grinned ruefully.

"Don't mind me, Dick," he said. "I'm in a bad mood, I guess."

Chapter 2

SPIDER LEGGETT had not had an easy road to his starting position as spread end for the Rams. He had played college football at the University of Houston, and he had been lucky that the Cougars, in his junior and senior years, had possessed the best passer in college football. Leggett had started as a running back, although at his weight, he could only be used in spots, even in college. He had, after his freshman year, tried to build himself up with a weight lifting program, hoping to reach at least 200 pounds.

But lifting weights only made him tired. His muscles grew harder, and he lifted more weight, but he gained only a few pounds. Resigned to the fact that his build was a naturally wiry one, he still hoped that his native speed and the elusiveness which had made him an all-state running back at San Antonio's Thomas Jefferson High School would make up for his 172-pound frame.

Midway through his sophomore year, when it had become apparent that the Houston sophomore quarterback had extraordinary potential as a passer, Flip Rudeen, the Cougar coach, had shifted Spider to spread end. The team went to an almost pure pro-type offense and for Spider, it had been a blessing.

In the next two seasons, he led the NCAA receivers in passes caught and was among the leaders in touchdowns scored and yards gained receiving. By the time he had finished his senior year at Houston, he fully expected to be one of the number one choices for pro football. He knew that many teams would be leary of his lack of size, but he felt that his performance over his last two seasons would make up for that.

He was taken on the sixth round by the Rams. By the time his name came up, he had almost given up hope that he would be drafted at all, even though he had filled out questionnaires for almost all the clubs in both the American and National Football Leagues and had talked to scouts from several teams. He had known that the Rams and the Houston Oilers were particularly interested in him, and he had half hoped that he would be taken by Houston. But he had made up his mind that he would go cheerfully to any club that drafted him.

The year that he was drafted, the Rams had two great ends in Hooks Terry and Jim Lyman, but Spider knew that both of them had been in the league a long time. Terry had just completed his tenth season and Lyman his ninth, and while

14

neither of them had tailed off much, he knew that after thirty, the life of a wide receiver was limited. Terry and Lyman could get by on their savvy for a while, but sometime in the next few years, the loss of speed would prove to be too much to make up for with guile.

So he had reported to the Ram training camp happily. The speed and reactions of the Ram defensive backs had come as a disagreeable shock to him.

He had spent that first training camp expecting the call of the Turk every night, after the club began cutting down to forty men. The moves that had freed him to catch so many passes in his college career were handled with almost contemptuous ease by the Ram defensive backs, and he was overawed by the skill and quickness of the two Ram veterans, Lyman and Terry. At night, after dinner and the team meeting, he studied his play book assiduously with an ear cocked for the knock on the door which would mean that an assistant coach had come to tell him that Steadman wanted to see him.

Each time the squad was cut, he was surprised to find that he was still on the team, and when the final cut was made and he was safe, he breathed a vast sigh of relief. He called his father, who was a high-school coach in Texas, and told him that this was the best night of his life, and his father laughed.

"I knew you'd make it, son," he said. "You've done everything else you ever set out to do."

"I never tried to do anything as tough as this before," Spider said, sincerely. "You don't know how good these guys are, Dad."

"You'll be a starter before the season ends, Ronald," his father said. "I'd bet on it." The only other person who ever called Spider Ronald, was his mother.

15

If his father had bet on it, he would have lost. Spider spent his rookie year watching the Rams win a championship from the worst seat in the parks they played in—the bench. He occasionally went in at the end of a game which had been wrapped up, or to relieve Terry or Lyman after they had run two long patterns in a row and were tired. He caught 11 passes for the year, but he felt that he had learned more about his trade in that one season than he had in the eight years he had played football in high school and college before.

When he came to camp for his second season with the Rams, he was not beset by the nagging fear of being cut each time the coaches met to trim the roster, but he began to wonder, halfway through the exhibition season, if he was ever going to get a chance to play first string. Steadman used him a good deal in the pre-season games, but he was never under the illusion that he was beating out either Lyman or Terry.

He worked with Red Dickey, the end coach, and began to understand the whole scheme of the pass patterns, rather than learning by rote the route he ran.

"You'll be a good end if you just learn your own patterns and run them as close to the way they are drawn as you can," Dickey explained to him one afternoon. "You've got speed to spare, and you have good hands. You still have a tendency to slow down a little when you make your cut, and you telegraph your last cut by making it more exaggerated than the early fakes, but you'll get out of that with time. But until you know the whole pattern and the routes the other receivers will run as well as you know your own, you won't be much help to the quarterback when a pattern breaks or the quarterback has to run for his life."

"I don't understand," Spider said.

"If you know where the other receivers are supposed t[o] you'll know where to go if you have time after you have your own pattern," Dickey said. "If Brad can't find an [o] receiver in the two and a half to three seconds he has, scramble. When he scrambles, if you don't know where other receivers are, all three of you might wind up in same spot. And you'll attract a crowd of defensive b[a] too."

"You mean I ought to work out another route after first one?"

"Improvise one," Dickey said. "Away from the othe[r] ceivers."

He made the club easily that year, and his post grad studies of football progressed. Once, riding with Dicke[y] a plane returning from a game with the Chicago Bear[s] screwed up his courage and asked the coach why he been taken so late in the draft.

Dickey looked at him and grinned.

"Don't feel bad," he said. "I was a twentieth. I figured drafted me just to have a warm body on hand to fill ou[t] scrimmages."

"But you were All-Pro," Spider said.

"Luckily, no one cares where you were drafted after get to camp," Dickey said. "When the head knocking s[t] the only thing that counts is how well you get the job [o] You did it well enough to stick."

"I thought I might go on the first round," Spider admi[tted] "I mean I had a pretty good college record."

"Lot better than pretty good," Dickey said. "But you a big strike against you on your size, Spider. Not many pound pro players around, even at spread end or flanke[r]

17

knew you had the speed and good enough moves, but you have to realize that by the time the pro season ends, we will have played more than twenty games. You have to be durable and we weren't sure enough of your durability to take a chance. The rest of the clubs felt the same way."

"I see," Spider said. "But I never was hurt in college, Red."

"You played eight, nine games a year and you didn't play against big, tough defensive backs every Saturday," Dickey said. "There's quite a difference."

"You said it," Spider said fervently. "There's quite a difference, all right."

By the end of his second season, he had caught twenty-eight passes, and he had played almost twice as many minutes as he had in his rookie season. Lyman and Terry needed more rest, and he was better able to replace either of them without cutting down on the efficiency of the Ram passing attack, but he knew that he did not approach either of them in all-around ability yet.

When Terry retired at the end of that second year, Spider felt that he was ready to move in as a starter, and he was determined to work even harder in training camp to prove that to the coaches. The Rams had drafted Gangel first, in the player selection meeting after the season, but Spider knew that this was insurance and that Gangel would not be a starter.

Lyman's injury forced Gangel into a starting role and made it certain that Spider himself would be a starter, but it made his job much more difficult, he discovered, as the season wore on. Even though Brad had almost quit throwing to him by the second half of the season, Spider still found that

in situations in which Brad had been apt to throw to him before, he was double covered.

The year before, when he had been in the game with either Lyman or Terry at the other wide receiver spot, the double coverage had automatically been on them. He found it more than twice as tough to break loose from the extra coverage because he never knew how it would be applied. Sometimes he would be covered short and deep, sometimes inside and out.

Early in the season, he worked assiduously at beating the double coverage and at recognizing what kind of coverage was used against him. As the passes thrown to him became fewer, he slacked off for a while, but then he grimly went back to working on the defensive backs even when he knew the ball would not be thrown in his direction.

He began keeping a book on the defensive backs, noting the patterns he felt he could beat each one on, checking to see which of them conceded the outside and which were inside conscious. Some backs played up tight, depending on their speeds for taking him deep, others—usually the slower ones—played farther back and were more likely to give him short passes to cut off the bombs.

He could determine their reactions even when Brad was not throwing to him, since the defensive backs never knew when he would get the ball and when he was purely a decoy. As the season went on, though, and it became more and more obvious that he was not the preferred receiver on the Ram team, he could sense a slackening by the defensive backs, so it became easier for him to beat them by a step or more. This only added to his frustration; knowing that he was open

19

often, he became more bitter when Thomas called patterns to the other receivers.

When the club reported for practice, at their Long Beach training camp, following the Falcon game, Spider, as usual, attended to his duties silently. He had been a talkative player the year before, full of chatter and spirit, but this year he had grown quieter as the weeks went by, and now he spoke only rarely, usually in answer to a suggestion by Dickey or a remark by Gangel or Billy Gallagher, the other deep receiver.

During practice, Thomas threw to him as often as he did to the other spread receivers, and Spider worked stolidly on refining his patterns. He seldom dropped the ball, but he knew that his performance during the week impressed no one. He had faltered under pressure, and he was beginning to believe that no one would ever forget it.

At the end of the long Tuesday afternoon workout, as he sat resting in the crowded dressing room, he reached a sudden decision. He had not thought of it before, but now it seemed imperative to him that if he were to be a successful pro, it would have to be on another team, where he could start fresh, without the stigma which had become attached to him here. He showered quickly, and dressed, and waited for Red Dickey to come out of the coaches' room. When Dickey came out, Spider stopped him.

"You got a few minutes, coach?"

Dickey nodded and looked at Spider curiously.

"Sure," he said. "I was just going up to the clubhouse to get a cup of coffee. Come along."

The Ram practice field during the season was located near a golf course and the coaches' office and meeting rooms were in the clubhouse. The club had only moved into this setup the year before, and it was still a little unfamiliar, although the facilities were far better than those the Rams had had before.

Spider and the coach walked across a parking lot, and up a winding road to the sprawling clubhouse, and into the small coffee shop, populated now by a few scattered golfers. After they had ordered their coffees, Dickey looked at him questioningly.

Spider stirred the coffee in his cup and stared down at the muddy brown liquid, searching for the proper words to say what he wanted to say.

"I want to be traded," he blurted out suddenly, not looking up. There was a long silence and finally he glanced up quickly to see Dickey sipping from his cup, his face thoughtful.

"It's too late to trade you this season," Dickey said. "We could put you on waivers, but I'm sure Steadman would not do that, and I don't think you would want it."

If Spider were put on waivers, he knew, he would be offered to the last place team in the league first, for the waiver price of $100. If no team in the league picked him up, he would become a free agent, but it was very unlikely that he would not be picked up. And it would be foolish for the Rams to put a first string offensive end on waivers when, by waiting until the end of the season, they could, at the very least, get a good draft choice for him.

"I know," Spider said.

"So why would you ask to be traded?"

Spider shook his head helplessly.

"I didn't think it out," he said. "I was sitting in the dressing

21

room trying to figure out what to do, and it just came to me; ask to be traded. I didn't know what the trade deadline was, but I'm not doing the Rams any good, and the Rams aren't doing me any good. I'd be a lot better off on another club, Red."

"I see," Dickey said. He tapped his spoon on the table thoughtfully for a while, watching Spider. The young man's face was clouded, and anger was beginning to cut through the desperation with which he had blurted out his desire to be traded.

"Why don't you put me on the bench?" Spider said fiercely. By now his mood had turned completely to anger, and he glared at the coach. "What good does it do for me to go out there and go through the motions on Sunday afternoon when you know, and I know, and every blasted defensive back in the league is beginning to know, that Brad won't throw to me?"

"He throws to you," Dickey said, mildly.

"Sure," Spider said, relieved by the chance to give his anger release. "Sure, he throws to me. When a pattern is busted or when he's running for his life, and he'd throw it up in the stands to keep from taking a loss. Then he throws to me. Me, Safety Valve Leggett."

"Have you talked to him about it?" Dickey asked him. "Brad's not a bad guy, Spider. You can't be a bad guy and be an All-Pro quarterback as often as he has. He's reasonable."

"I haven't talked to him," Spider said, flatly. He had considered approaching Thomas, but had never been able to decide upon a reasonable approach.

"Why not?"

22

"I'm no motor mouth," Spider said. "I'm not going to run crying to Thomas and ask him to throw to me. He knows I get open. He sees the same movies I do."

"He's also aware that you've dropped some passes under pressure," Dickey said bluntly. "I suppose you know that, too."

The harsh truth hit Spider like a dash of cold water, and his anger suddenly fled.

"That's right, coach," he said miserably. "I guess you can't really blame him. That's why I want to be traded. I'd be better off with a fresh start."

Dickey glanced at his watch and stood up. He put a hand on Spider's shoulder, and when the end looked up, he grinned at him.

"Ease up," he said. "Maybe we can work something out. You're too tense, Spider. Remember one thing, son. You're still our number one spread end. You'll get a shot again. Hang tough."

Chapter 3

SPIDER drove slowly from the practice field to his apartment on the outskirts of Long Beach. He felt drained and tired, not only from the physical demands of the long practice, but from the emotional release of his outburst to Red Dickey. He could not see that he had solved anything. Certainly the Rams would not trade him now, or put him on waivers. All he had accomplished was to make sure that they would trade him next year.

He parked his car and walked into the small apartment. It was late afternoon, and the living room was dark, so he snapped on the table lamp by the big leather easy chair which was the one extravagance he had allowed himself in buying furniture.

He had picked up a paper on his way in, and he dropped into the chair and opened it automatically. He stared at it for a long time before he realized he was not reading it.

He dropped the paper and walked into the small kitchen; he opened the refrigerator and took out a large steak. He heated a heavy iron skillet, sprinkling its surface with coarse-grained salt, and when it was very hot and the salt had just begun to brown, he dropped the heavy steak on it. It sizzled and smoked, and he opened the window to let the smoke out. After a few moments, he turned the steak, noting with satis-faction that the underside had browned and crisped. He liked steak blood rare on the inside and crisp and dark brown on the outside, and, after a couple of minutes, this one met his specifications.

He sliced a big beef tomato, got out a plate, and sat down to his lonely dinner, his mind now busy again with the prob-lem of his job with the Rams. He ate the steak slowly, trying to determine where he had gone wrong, what had made him drop passes in game action, whether he really heard foot-steps when he turned for the ball. He decided at last, certain of his own courage, that the footsteps had never been a fac-tor.

When he had finished the steak, he washed the dish, wiped the frying pan, and went back to the leather chair. He picked up the paper again, but when he opened it to the sports page and settled himself to read, the face of Brad Thomas came between him and the printed page. It was a good, strong face, open and friendly, but for Spider it brought only anger and a deep sense of injustice.

He threw the paper down and jumped to his feet, anger again washing over him. Dickey had suggested that he talk to Thomas about his problem, and now he decided that it could do no harm.

Might even help, he thought wryly. He went to his desk and found the list of players' addresses and phone numbers provided by the club to all players. He knew Brad lived in Long Beach, not far away, and he found the address and the telephone number quickly.

He hesitated after he picked up the phone and had begun to dial. For a brief moment, he wondered what he would say to Brad, how he would explain his feelings. Then he finished dialing quickly, and when he heard Thomas answer the phone, he said abruptly, "Brad, this is Spider. I want to see you."

At the other end of the wire there was a short silence, then Brad, surprised, "Is it important? Tiny and I were just about to go to a movie."

"It's important to me," Spider said, doggedly.

"Hold on a minute," Brad said. Spider could hear him talking for a moment, then he came back.

"How long will this take?" he asked.

"Not long," Spider said. He had already begun to regret the call, but he could not back out now.

"Can't we handle it on the telephone?" Brad asked.

"I'd rather talk to you in person," Spider said.

"Okay," Brad said, resignedly. "Why don't you come on over?"

"I'd like to talk to you alone, if I can," Spider said. "This is just between the two of us."

"Tiny can go eat a banana split," Brad said and laughed. "He's always ready to do that."

"Thanks," Spider told him and hung up. He was surprised

27

to find that he was gripping the telephone with all his strength and that his palms were wet. He made a conscious effort to relax, and put the telephone gently back in its cradle.

Brad and Tiny Ross shared a big apartment about five miles from Spider's place, on the beach in an area made up of luxury homes and apartments. On the drive to their place, Spider tried to go over in his mind an opening remark, but by the time he parked, he was still at a loss.

As he started to ring the bell at the apartment door, it opened and Ross, the massive defensive tackle for the Rams who had come up in his rookie season with Thomas and had roomed with him ever since, came out.

"Hey, Spider," he said, his wide face creased with a warm smile. "Got problems? Ol' Brad'll take care of them for you, hoss. See you later."

Brad was in the living room, and he waved at Spider to come in, his face friendly but puzzled.

"Sit down," he said. "How about a beer?"

"That's fine," Spider said. "I'd like a beer."

He sat down and fidgeted while Brad went out to the kitchen and came back with two cans of cold beer. He handed one to Spider and sipped appreciatively from the other.

"Funny thing," he said. "I don't drink much beer, but once in a long while a cold one tastes real good. I think it's after a long workout on a hot afternoon, like today. Guess I get hydrated—or dehydrated."

Spider took a gulp of beer, swallowed wrong, and coughed helplessly. Brad came over to him, and slapped him hard on the back two or three times, and waited until the coughing had subsided, and Spider was sitting back, trying to get his breath.

28

"Went down your Sunday throat," Brad said. "I do that now and then."

Spider watched Thomas while he struggled to get control of his voice and breath. He felt stupid and clumsy and regretted having come, but he knew that he would never forgive himself if he did not go through with his plan, so finally he spoke.

"Look," he said. "I didn't come over to drink beer, Brad. I have to talk to you about something."

"I suspected as much," Brad said, dryly.

Spider was quiet for a long while, twisting the beer can in his hands and staring at it, groping for the right words.

"I don't want to sound like a sorehead or a crybaby," he said at last. "And I don't think I'm the best pass receiver to come down the pike since Elroy Hirsch or Tom Fears. What I want to say, I guess, is I'm a better receiver than you seem to think I am, and you ought to throw to me more."

The last few words came out in a rush, and when he had spoken them, Spider leaned back in relief. He looked at Thomas, and the Ram quarterback was studying his can of beer now.

Brad started to speak, but Spider thought of something else he had wanted to say.

"Look," he said, more sure of himself, "I know I dropped a couple of balls early in the season, Brad, but I guess it was more nerves than anything else. It wasn't footsteps. No one has ever accused me of hearing footsteps, Brad. You know that."

Thomas put his beer down on the coffee table and stood up. He walked to the big picture window which looked out on the ocean and stood there, for what seemed a long time to Spider, contemplating the rapidly darkening Pacific Ocean.

When he finally turned back to look at Spider, his face was very serious.

"I don't know if you hear footsteps or not, Spider," he said. "I certainly have never said I thought you did. I figure anyone your size who plays football has to have guts or he wouldn't be on the ball club. This isn't a game for cowards, and I don't know any cowards playing it."

"So why don't you throw me the ball?" Spider broke in. "Hell, you can see me open, Brad. You know I can beat single coverage, and I can beat double coverage too, if I have to."

Brad held up his hand to silence the younger player.

"I know that," he said. "I know you get open, Spider. I know you work on the defensive backs even when you're not the primary receiver, and I know you're developing into one of the best fakers in the business. But I can't gamble on throwing to you, Spider."

"Why?" Spider cried out. "Why? Just because I dropped a few balls? You going to hold that against me the rest of my life?"

"No," Brad said. "It's hard to explain, Spider, but I'll try."

He sat down, drank from his can of beer, and stared out the window, gathering his thoughts. Spider watched him tensely, sitting on the edge of his chair, squeezing the can between his hands.

"I know how you must feel," Brad said, slowly. "I don't know how many balls you dropped in the first two or three games, Spider, but I know when you dropped them. You cost two or three touchdowns and two or three first downs, and you can't give up points or the ball that often in this league without losing games. If you lose enough games, you lose the championship."

"It's not all my fault," Spider said, desperately. "I'm not the only guy on the club who makes mistakes. I've seen Grut miss blocks and Shrake drop the ball, and I've even seen you fumble. You aren't perfect."

"I'd be the first to agree with you on that," Thomas said ruefully. "I'm a long way from perfect, Spider. But at the moment, I'm the only quarterback the coaches figure should run the club, so they put up with my faults. One of the reasons they put up with me is that they trust my judgment on calls and on passes, Spider. And right now, in my judgment, I can't afford to gamble a million dollars on you in a clutch situation."

"A million bucks!" Spider said indignantly. "How can it cost a million bucks to throw me one stinking pass?"

"Figure it out," Brad said, patiently. "We haven't got the division championship sewed up, and we'll be lucky if we win it, Spider. The season's half over, and the tough half of the schedule is coming up. I remember one year we lost a championship on one ball dropped in the end zone, and I guess if you wanted to go over any season with any club that finished a game out, you could find one or two plays that made the difference."

"Maybe so," Spider said doubtfully. "But I still don't see how it costs a million bucks to throw to me, Brad."

"Then listen," Brad said. "If we win the division championship and play the champions of the Central Division for the Western Conference championship, that means an extra-game salary for every player. The Rams have a high salary budget,

31

so I would guess that averages out to about eighteen hundred dollars each for forty guys. Right?"

"Right," Spider said.

"We win that and go on to the NFL championship game," Brad said. "That's in the East this year, which means we'd be playing in a big stadium before up to eighty-two thousand, if Cleveland wins, and the winner's share of that game could come to about nine thousand dollars per player. That adds up to three hundred sixty thousand dollars plus seventy-two thousand dollars for the division playoff. That's what? My addition's off tonight."

"I figure four hundred thirty-two thousand bucks," Spider said.

"Then add fifteen thousand dollars per player for Super Bowl if we could win that and you come up with six hundred thousand dollars more or a total of a million thirty-two thousand," Brad said. "You begin to understand why I can't take unnecessary chances, Spider?"

"I never thought of it that way," Spider said, impressed in spite of himself. "But it can't all ride on my dropping one or two passes, Brad. How do you know I won't catch the ball in the clutch now?"

"I don't know you'll drop the ball," Thomas admitted. "And I guess if I had been throwing to you for a long time, Spider, I'd take a chance that the balls you dropped early were flukes. But unluckily for you, I spent quite a few years throwing to Hooks and Jim Lyman, and I never knew one of them to drop a clutch ball. So when you dropped a series of them, I had to give up on you. I just can't afford the chance, Spider."

Spider got up and looked down at Thomas. The anger and

frustration came back in a rush, and he slammed down the beer can and turned to the door.

"Thanks," he said. "I drop a few balls, and Brad Thomas, the Golden Arm and the judge, decides that he can't throw to me any more because it might cost him a payoff. You don't know that's true, you just think it may be true because a couple of your old buddies aren't on the club any more, and you just can't stand trusting any one else. I asked Red Dickey to see about trading me today, Brad. I hope he can work something out when the season is over. Even if I caught a hundred passes in the next seven games, I wouldn't want to play with a self-righteous hypocrite like you."

He opened the door and turned back to say something else.

"You'll cost the club the championship a lot quicker by not throwing to me," he went on. "Every club in the league knows how you feel now, big shot. They use single coverage on me, and before long, I bet they start playing me loose so that the guy on me can drop off or come up against the run. What'll you do then, Golden Arm? Run the ball yourself?"

Thomas started to reply, but Spider slammed the door and walked rapidly to his car. He got in and burned rubber as he pulled away from the curb, still possessed by a deep, strong anger.

By the time he reached his own apartment, parked, and sat down again in the big leather chair, the first flush of rage had worn off, and he began to have second thoughts about his confrontation with Thomas. He thought about the things he had said and grew more and more dejected.

He probably won't ever throw the ball to me again, Spider thought. By the time he thinks over all the things I said, he'll ask Steadman to put me on the bench. If I ever had a chance to catch the ball, I just blew it.

Me. Me, telling Brad Thomas what a great receiver I am. Telling the best quarterback in pro football how to run a game. And all I ever did for this club was drop passes my baby sister could catch. They will put me on waivers tomorrow or maybe tonight if Brad calls Coach.

The phone rang and he paid no attention to it in his deep despair. It was not until it had rung for a long time that he picked it up.

"Hey, Spider," Tiny Ross said. "What's with you and the Golden Arm?"

"What do you mean?"

"Look," Tiny said. "You're a nice guy, Spider. I don't know you real well since you play on the glory squad, but I want to know what you did to upset Brad, baby. We win with him."

"Upset him?"

"That's right," Tiny said. "We were supposed to go to a movie, and I come back from eating a banana split, and he tells me he don't feel like going out, and he won't tell me what you guys talked about. What gives?"

"Nothing," Spider said. "We just talked about pass patterns."

"Look," Tiny said, and Spider wondered if he started every sentence with the same word. "Look. This club depends on Brad for a lot, buddy. It don't depend on you for nothing. If you got troubles, keep them. He don't need them."

"Hey," Spider cried. "I didn't . . ."

"I hope you didn't," Tiny said. "If you think you had troubles before, you just beginning."

34

The click of the receiver was loud in Spider's ear, and he put the telephone down slowly. At first he was disturbed by the call, then a slow anger began to burn in him, fed by frustration and by the knowledge that he was a better football player than anyone—Dickey, Thomas, Ross or any of the others—gave him credit for being.

I'll show the so-and-sos, he thought. I'll show them.

If I get a chance.

Chapter 4

He was apprehensive the next morning when he got up to prepare to go to practice. He liked to leave his apartment in time to have breakfast in a small restaurant nearby, eating bacon and eggs and grapefruit and cereal while he read the morning sports page. This morning the food seemed tasteless, and he found it difficult to concentrate on the column Jack Oslen, the veteran sports columnist for the *Los Angeles Times*, had written about the prospects for the club for the rest of the season.

Oslen, as usual, took a rather dim view of the Ram chances. Spider knew the long, thin writer casually. A few times, after Spider had had an exceptionally good day and once, after he had dropped the big passes, Oslen had fixed him with his black, owlish eyes, peering through horn-rimmed glasses and asked him a few pertinent questions. His quotes had been accurate, at least.

The column was headed "Can the Rams Move on Three Legs?"

As Spider waited for the waitress to bring his order, he began to read without real interest, but his interest grew quickly.

"The Rams have established a strong bid for another championship in the National Football League," Oslen began. "This is not surprising, although the personnel has changed markedly and Steadman, a man who is not fond of playing rookies in his starting lineups, is using more than the Rams have used since 1949. But this crop of rookies is nearly as talented as that 1949 group, which included Vitamin Smith, Tommy Kalmanir, Tank Younger, Jerry Williams, Norman Van Brocklin, and a few more who went on to full-fledged stardom as pros."

The waitress brought Spider's cereal, and he poured milk on the Corn Flakes and began to eat. He had eaten two spoonfuls, while reading, before he realized he had forgotten to add sugar.

"What is surprising," Oslen went on, "is that the Rams have done so well so far, operating on seven cylinders. It may be a far-fetched analogy to compare a football team to an eight-cylinder automobile engine, but it is a valid one. Pro football clubs operate in eight areas of competence, and the great pro football clubs click on all eight.

"On defense, the motivating forces are a defensve line, linebackers, and defensive backs. The Rams have these three cylinders turning over at full horsepower. Then there's the kicking game, and the rookie punter, Boomer Terrell, has been averaging 46 yards a punt to lead the league. Another rookie, Rockie Stebbins, has replaced the retired veteran, Stan Smith, more than adequately on field goals."

Spider finished his cereal and did not look up as the girl slid the plate of bacon and eggs in front of him. She asked if he wanted coffee with the meal, and he shook his head no.

"On offense," Oslen's column went on, "the Rams are only hitting well on three of the four cylinders. The runners are strong and fast and, for the most part, experienced. Bob Ottum, Flash Werner, and Skeeter Tilson are three of the best veteran backs in the league, and Squirmin' Herman Weiskopf and Rabbit Laguerre are two of the most promising first-year men.

"Slats Shrake and Earl Burton provide unusual size and speed at tight end, and Shrake should be All-Pro again this year. Dick Gangel, who has replaced Hooks Terry as the Ram flanker, may not be All-Pro, but he'll be in contention for Rookie of the Year, if he continues to improve. Brad Thomas, who has been All-Pro for three years now, uses these tools with all the consummate skill which marks him as a quarterback.

"But there is a blind spot—or a missing cylinder, to keep the analogy alive—in the Ram attack. If it isn't repaired or tuned up, the Rams' promising first half may be wasted in a disastrous second half. You can't win in this league on a faulty performance."

Spider looked up as the waitress asked, "Coffee now?" He nodded and went back to the column.

"Since the third game of the season," Oslen wrote, "Thomas has almost completely ignored Spider Leggett as a target in the Ram passing attack. Leggett dropped passes in those first three games, to be sure. So did other Ram receivers. But Thomas has not quit throwing to the other receivers, and he has given up on Leggett. He won't say so, because we have asked him, but he has obviously lost confidence in Leggett.

"That, of course, is his business and the business of the Ram coaches. But it must be as obvious to them as it is to us that you can't shut off one receiver entirely and expect your offense to work."

Spider nodded, and the waitress, misunderstanding, poured him another cup of coffee. He looked up at her in surprise and said "Thanks."

"If Leggett can't get the job done, the Rams better replace him," the column went on. "If he can, then Thomas better start throwing to him. The defenses in the league are already beginning to ignore him, and it is getting harder for Thomas to complete passes to the tight end or the spread end. Gangel is a rookie, and when he gets double coverage every Sunday, his effectiveness is destroyed. Shrake can't carry the whole load at tight end.

"Thomas has been throwing more and more to his running backs to ease the squeeze on the two other receivers he uses, but that's only a stopgap measure. We don't know what the problem with Leggett is, but if the Rams do not solve it and solve it soon, they are headed for trouble."

"You want another cup?" the waitress said, looking at Spider unbelievingly. "That's four."

"Four?"

"Usually you have two."

"I guess I'm thirsty."

40

She poured another cup of coffee, and Spider stirr[ed] without looking at it.

"We don't know whether Leggett is the answer or [not,]" Oslen wrote. "But he has speed, and last season he de[mon-]strated that he has great hands. It seems to this obser[ver] bit premature for Thomas or for the coaches to quit on [him] on the basis of three or four dropped passes. When he [was] going well last year, the Rams thought he would be the [best] Tommy McDonald in the league. We think he might [still] be if Thomas will throw to him.

"How about it, Brad?"

Spider put the paper down and was surprised when [he] looked at his watch and found that he would have to h[urry] to make the dressing room and the morning meeting on ti[me.] He left money for the waitress and trotted out to his [car,] and as he drove the short blocks to the Ram practice field[, he] went over Oslen's column in his mind. Oslen had said m[any] of the things he had been thinking for the last six weeks, [and] some of the things he had said to Brad the evening bef[ore.] He wondered what had inspired the columnist to write [in] this vein at just this time.

He was still preoccupied, when he parked the car a[nd] walked into the crowded dressing room. He did not not[ice] that most of the players ignored him as he sat down in fr[ont] of his locker and began unlacing his shoes. He had alw[ays] been a loner, and Gangel was still the only really close frie[nd] he had on the club.

But by the time he had stripped, and put on his pa[nts,] shoes, and T-shirt, and gone into the room for the offens[ive] team meeting, he began to be aware that the silence towa[rd] him was more pronounced than it had ever been before. [He]

41

looked around curiously, but none of the players returned his glance, and he shrugged and concentrated on making notes in his play book on the shadings and changes in the offense for the game coming up.

When the meeting ended, he put on his pads and shirt, picked his helmet up by the face bar, and trooped out to the field with the rest of the club. He was not particularly disturbed by the silence of the other players toward him; occasionally the team was caught up in tension early in the week before a game, and since they were playing Green Bay on Sunday, he could understand. Green Bay was always a formidable team, and this season was no exception.

He was still thinking about Oslen's column and about his conversation with Thomas when Thomas called the first pattern in the offensive drill. It was a pass to Spider, and he ran the pattern crisply and stretched easily to take the ball in.

It slapped into his hands, and he tucked it away under his arm and ran the pattern out, faking the defensive safety. As he trotted back toward the line of scrimmage, Dick Jones, the safety, looked at him and said, "Slow down, show boat. Oslen's not out here today."

Spider glanced at him in surprise, thinking that he was kidding, but Jones's face was hard and unfriendly. Leggett shrugged and went back to the offensive side of the line. Gallagher would run this pattern, but Spider listened to the call anyway. The pass was a quick look-in to the tight end, and Frog Howard, taking his turn at quarterback, drilled the ball hard into the big receiver's arms.

Spider moved back in for his turn and was surprised when Thomas called another deep pattern to him. Again he ran the pattern well, broke free and had to pour on speed to reach

the ball, which seemed to him a bit overthrown. Still, he reached it and made a fingertip catch.

This time Jones did not say anything to him as he came back upfield, and Spider decided he must have been kidding the first time. He was back at spread end, with Gallagher now relieving Gangel at flanker back, and he was puffing slightly as he leaned in for the signal. He had run all out for fifty yards twice in the last minute and trotted back farther, and he could feel it.

"XY corner," Brad said. "Tight slant, total block. Brown, on three."

Again the pattern would send Spider deep downfield, and this time as he raced along the sideline before cutting on an angle toward the corner of the field at the opposite sideline, he could feel the beginning of real tiredness in his legs and in his shortness of breath. The ball was thrown ahead of him, and only by making a diving catch did he manage to reach it this time. He lay for a moment sprawled on the grass, trying to catch his breath.

Jones looked down at him and said, "Come on, motor mouth. You want to catch passes, don't you?"

Spider scrambled to his feet, his temper beginning to go, but he stopped himself in time and trotted slowly back to where the offensive team was waiting. He should get a rest this time; the deep receivers, with three of them working, ran only two out of three plays.

"Come on," Steadman called to him impatiently. "Hurry up. We haven't got all day."

Surprised, Spider broke into a run, looking for Gallagher as he reached the huddle. The rookie substitute was not in sight, and he listened angrily as Brad called still another long pass.

The rest of the afternoon passed as a long, grim nightmare for the young receiver. Thomas could not call all long passes; the club had to work on other phases of the offense, as well. But he called them as often as he could, and Gallagher did not return to the practice field. Spider was too stubborn to ask what had happened to the rookie so he ran out his patterns as hard as he could despite his growing weariness and the fire that began to burn in his chest as he fought for air.

At last it ended, and Spider walked grimly back to the dressing room. His legs ached, and it was a long time before he could breathe easily. He sat slumped before his locker gathering his strength and trying to control his temper when Thomas stopped and looked down at him, coldly.

"You didn't feel neglected out there today, did you?" he asked.

"No," Spider said. "Thanks."

"You won't feel it necessary to complain to your friend Oslen that we are mistreating you?"

Leggett looked up at the quarterback in surprise.

"I don't know Oslen," he said.

"You must have read his column this morning," Brad said. "Didn't you?"

"I read it."

"Where do you suppose he got it?"

"I don't suppose he 'got it' anywhere," Spider said. He was growing more and more angry, and he forced himself to calm down. "Maybe he just figured it out for himself."

Thomas was quiet as he stared down at Spider, and Spider met his gaze defiantly. The rest of the dressing room had

44

grown quiet enough so that he could hear the voices of the coaches talking as they undressed in their room.

"Maybe," Thomas said at last. "Funny he should just figure it out for himself right after you come to complain to me about neglecting you."

"What do you mean?" Spider said, the anger beginning to take over. "You saying I called Oslen and complained to him?"

He stood up, dropping his helmet, and glared at Thomas. The quarterback was three or four inches taller, and Spider had to look up into the cold gray eyes which surveyed him with what he felt was contempt.

"I didn't say anything like that," Thomas said. He started to turn away, then looked back. "You looked good out there today, motor mouth," he said. "But then we weren't tackling."

He started to turn away again, and Spider lost the small vestige of control he had left. All the frustration of the last few weeks boiled up in him, and he swung the bigger man around, hauling violently on his jersey.

"You think I'm gutless?" he yelled and swung wildly, his fist glancing off the side of Thomas's head. He swung again and this time had the satisfaction of landing solidly on Brad's jaw, but the blow did not stagger Thomas. As Spider started another roundhouse right hand, he felt an explosive, numbing shock on his jaw and fell.

When he came to, he was still on the floor, but no one was paying any attention to him. He could feel the chill of the concrete against his cheek, and he lifted his head groggily. He was lying on his stomach, and for a few moments he could not understand how he had gotten there.

As his head cleared, he remembered the fight with Thomas

45

and tried to scramble quickly to his feet, but his legs were shaky, and he had to sit down on the stool in front of his locker, quickly, to keep from falling. He sat with his head hanging for what seemed a long time, before he regained his senses fully.

Then he realized that the dressing room was deserted, and he wondered how long he had lain on the floor. Bitterness welled up in him when he thought that the players, and trainers, and coaches had left him lying there. He wondered what had hit him and stood slowly, feeling his jaw. It was tender and beginning to swell.

As he explored the damage gingerly, he became aware of hushed voices coming from the training room and walked in that direction to find the team crowded into the area around the rubbing tables and whirlpool baths. The Ram team doctor was examining Thomas, feeling gently the bones of his right hand, and the players were watching anxiously.

Spider's head ached, but it was clear, and he began to realize that Thomas had knocked him out with a right to the chin. He had heard that Thomas was a fighter; one of the legends of the Ram quarterback was the epic fight he had had with Flash Werner early in his career.

"Hurt there?" the doctor asked Thomas, probing carefully.

The big quarterback winced and nodded.

"Anything broken?" he asked, and the players hung in hushed apprehension on the answer.

The doctor probed again, and again Thomas winced.

"We'll have to X-ray," the doctor said. "I'm afraid there is a break there, Brad. Let's make sure, though."

"What does that mean, Doc?" Steadman asked. The massive coach watched the doctor's face worriedly. "How long will he be out if the knuckle is broken?"

The doctor shrugged unhappily.

"At least a month," he said. "Could be six weeks before he can throw well again, if there's a fracture."

Chapter 5

THE doctor turned to lead Brad out of the room to take him for X-rays and saw Spider, who was standing, thunderstruck, at the back of the small crowd of players. As he turned, the players turned with him and suddenly Spider found himself the target of the angry scrutiny of the whole group.

There was a long moment of silence, then Dr. Fisher pushed his way past the players and stopped in front of Spider.

He reached up and felt Spider's jaw, moving it from side to side carefully. "Bite down," he commanded, and Leggett automatically clenched his jaws.

"No harm done." Dr. Fisher said. He looked at Spider for

a moment, then shook his head abruptly. "Worse luck," he added and stalked away.

Thomas and the coaches followed him out of the room and the only sound was Thomas's cleats on the cement floor. The players were still staring at Spider; finally he turned slowly, and went back to his locker, and sat down. The doctor had put a sideline cape over Thomas's shoulders, and the quarterback left with the doctor and coaches without taking time to change into his street clothes.

When they had gone, the other players trooped back into the locker room. They dispersed to their lockers silently, a few of them glancing angrily toward Spider, but none of them had anything to say to him. When conversation started, it was concerned with the seriousness of the injury to Brad's hand. Spider had the eerie feeling that he had been wiped out of the consciousness of the club and that he was, in fact, invisible.

He undressed slowly and went into the shower, the only player there for a few minutes. He finished showering quickly and returned to get into his street clothes, dressing rapidly, anxious only to get out of the room and away from the other men.

He had almost finished when Marty Nathan, the squat, powerful offensive guard who was an offensive team captain, came over to him. The fact that Nathan was clad only in a towel draped around his middle, did nothing to detract from his dignity or the menace in his manner as he stopped in front of Spider.

"You may have cost this ball club a championship, mouth," he said bluntly. "I'm not the coach or the general manager, or I'd bounce you out of here so fast you'd burn rubber for a block trying to stop. You've had it, mouth. You talk all you want from now on. No one will listen and no one will talk back."

Spider stared at him stupidly, trying to comprehend what he was saying. His jaw had begun to throb, and he could not think clearly, and finally he turned away wordlessly and walked out into the open air. He was surprised to find the late afternoon sun still shining. It seemed to him that hours had passed since the end of practice, and it should be night.

When he reached his apartment, he tried to read the afternoon papers to get his mind off the disastrous afternoon. He thought of calling Dr. Fisher to find out what had happened to Brad's hand, but decided that he better not. He did not know if the team ban on talking to him extended to the doctor or not, but he did not want to find out.

When the telephone rang, he jumped, then answered warily.

Steadman's voice was unemotional and businesslike.

"Come into my office tomorrow morning, Leggett," he said flatly. "I would like to talk to you."

"Yes, sir," Spider said. "How is Brad's hand?"

"Broken," Steadman replied, and the click of the phone being hung up seemed as loud as an explosion in Spider's ear.

That does it, he thought, replacing the receiver. That really wraps it up. Maybe I can catch on somewhere in the American Football League. There must be a club that needs a receiver.

He slept only briefly that night. When he finally got out of bed at the first sign of light, he felt stiff and sore all over and wondered why, until he remembered the tough workout

Thomas had given him. He felt his jaw and found that it was much more swollen and very tender, and when he looked at his face in the mirror preparing to shave, he saw a puffy, blue-red swelling on the left side of the jaw. He grinned ruefully as he lathered gently.

Leave it to me, he thought. I got to pick the hardest punching quarterback in football to jump. I'm lucky he didn't knock all my teeth out.

His mind was clear now, and some of the shock of the situation had worn off. He was sure that the Rams would put him on waivers; even if they were hard up for deep receivers, they could not afford to keep a troublemaker who had injured their number one quarterback.

He ate his breakfast cheerfully. He could not imagine anything worse happening, and he felt almost relief that his problem had been settled. There was nothing he could do to affect the decision of Steadman or the Ram head office, so he could cast out his fears and frustrations and relax.

The headline in the *Times* sports section was on Brad's injury, naturally enough. Spider had not considered how Jack Teale, the Ram publicity man, would handle the story. He knew that Teale could not say that the injury had come from Thomas punching spread end Spider Leggett on his cement head.

He had not eaten dinner the night before, and he found that he was, all at once, ravenously hungry. He ordered a breakfast steak, a double order of eggs and toast and the usual cereal, and devoured a grapefruit while he waited.

The *Times* lead had been written by Oslen. Spider surmised that Teale had called the sports writer with his version of what had happened, after being briefed by Steadman on what to say.

"Ram hopes for another NFL championship may have been shattered on the hard tile floor of the shower of the club's Long Beach training camp yesterday evening," the story began. "Brad Thomas, for the last three years All-Pro quarterback of the club, slipped and broke a knuckle in his right hand after practice. Dr. Martin Fisher, the team doctor, has placed the Ram star's hand in a cast, but he says that Thomas will be out of action for at least a month and that he will probably be unable to throw effectively for six weeks or longer.

"If Thomas is out for the next six weeks, that means that the Rams must finish the season without him," Oslen went on. "Frog Howard is a fine quarterback. Many experts consider him the best backup quarterback in football and he may very well be. But you don't win championships with backup quarterbacks and if the Rams must do without Thomas, the chances of their repeating as champions are almost nil."

The story went on to detail Frog's performance over the last several years on the occasions he had been called upon to replace Brad. Overall, his performance had been good, but Oslen had a reservation about his ability to carry the entire load of the Ram offense over a length of time.

"There is a tremendous difference between being the backup quarterback and the number one," he wrote. "It may seem strange that a quarterback who can come in late in a game and do well, or who can take over a club for two or three games and do well, cannot take the same club over a season and do just as well.

"But it is true that some quarterbacks are not temperamentally capable of carrying the burden of command for a whole season or for half a season. It may be that they cannot take the sustained pressure or it may be that the club itself, knowing that they must make it without their usual leader, becomes nervous and inefficient. Howard has done well enough for short stints. The history of clubs who have had to depend too heavily on their number twos is that they usually founder. Until Howard has shown his ability to stand up under the pressures he will be subject to, the prognosis for the Rams is the same as the prognosis for Brad's hand—bad."

Spider finished his breakfast and ordered more coffee, prompting the waitress to smile and say, "You getting to be a real coffee head, Spider."

He smiled back at her.

"Coffee is getting better," he said. "You must be making it."

"Me? All I can make is instant coffee."

He laughed as she walked away from him and was surprised that he felt so relaxed. He was not even concerned with the interview coming up with Steadman. He looked at his watch and saw that it was still early enough for him to enjoy his coffee at leisure.

As he sipped the coffee, he thought of what he would say to Steadman. On sober afterthought, he had been wrong to swing at Thomas, but no one could blame him for the broken hand. He hadn't hit Brad in the hand with his jaw, he thought, and grinned. The grin hurt.

The waitress was back with the coffee pot, but he shook his head. She looked at him curiously as he paid the check.

"You been in a fight?" she asked.

"No," Spider said. "I fell down in the bath tub."

"Really hit yourself a lick," she said sympathetically. "Funny you play pro football and all that, then get hurt in the bath tub."

"Real funny," Spider said.

He parked in the small lot outside the clubhouse and stopped for a minute to look out over the golf course toward the field where the Rams worked out. It seemed strange that he might not be there later and for a flash, he felt a deep depression, but it passed as quickly as it had come, and he had returned to his mood of cheerful fatalism by the time he was climbing the stairs to Steadman's office.

He knocked on the door firmly and Steadman's voice came at once.

"Spider?"

Spider opened the door and walked in and was surprised to find that he was not nervous. Most of the time, when Steadman called a player in alone, it was cause for a nervous breakdown.

The big coach looked up at him somberly and pointed to the one chair in the small room.

"Sit," he said.

Spider sat down and crossed his legs and Steadman leaned back in the ancient swivel chair behind his deck. The chair creaked dangerously, but held up.

"What happened?" the coach asked, his eyes fixed steadily on Spider's.

"I don't know," Spider said. "I didn't see the punch, I guess. One minute I was up, fighting, the next thing I knew I woke up on the floor, and everyone was gone."

"I don't mean the fight," Steadman said impatiently. "Brad told me about that. He hit you with a sucker right hand. I told him he should have left hooked you and saved his right hand, but he said he wasn't thinking. What started it?"

Spider looked down at the floor and tried to gather his thoughts and find a way to tell Steadman in a few words what had started it. The long afternoons of frustration, and the hours he had spent thinking about it, and the passes he had dropped, and the passes that Thomas had not thrown to him all flashed through his mind, but he knew that he could not explain how all of this had built up inside him.

"It's hard to say," he got out finally. "A lot of things, coach. What difference does it make?" Since he knew that Steadman had called him in to get rid of him, he saw no real reason for trying to go over the long list of things which had culminated in his swinging at Thomas.

Steadman regarded him steadily for what seemed to Spider like a very long time, his strong face expressionless and his right leg pumping rapidly up and down. Spider knew that the active leg indicated anger, even if Steadman's face did not show it.

"Leggett, I don't understand you," Steadman grated. "What is the matter with you?"

"The matter with me?"

"You. You're a guy with speed, hands, talent, and I used to think you had the desire to make a great receiver. What happened?"

"Nothing," Spider said. He was losing the detachment which had protected him when he had entered the office. "Nothing happened to me, coach. I dropped a couple of balls, and Thomas forgot me."

56

"He told me about that," Steadman said. "You came over to his place and hollered about it."

"I didn't holler," Spider said. "All I wanted to know was why he didn't throw to me. I get open all day, and he throws to Gangel or Shrake. I didn't drop balls last year, coach. I won't drop them this year, if he'll throw to me."

"He won't be throwing to you," Steadman said.

The anger left Spider suddenly as he remembered why he was in Steadman's office.

"I guess not," he said. "When do I leave?"

"Leave?"

"Leave," Spider repeated. "You must have put me on waivers by now. Has anybody claimed me?"

"You're not on waivers," Steadman said. "I wish you were, Leggett. I guess you haven't heard about Gallagher."

"I read about Brad," Spider said, puzzled. "I didn't see anything about Gallagher. What's wrong with him?"

"He's got mononucleosis," Steadman said. "Didn't you notice he left practice yesterday?"

"I noticed he didn't run any patterns," Spider said bitterly. "I ran every long pattern in the book all afternoon."

"You had that coming, too," Steadman told him. "Thomas told me about you calling Oslen to complain, and I told him it was all right to wear you out a little, Leggett."

"I didn't call Oslen," Spider said desperately. "I don't know Oslen that well." He stood up and started to leave, anxious to get out of the room and away from Steadman and the rest of the Rams.

"Look," he said. "I'm not on waivers yet, so put me on. I've had it here, coach. The players don't like me, you figure I'm some kind of kook, and I made the real big mistake of hitting

57

the Golden Arm on the fist with my head. So there's no point in my jawing about it. Goodbye and good luck."

He started to open the door, and Steadman called to him. "You stay here," he roared and Spider stopped. "Shut the door, and come back, and sit down and listen, big mouth."

Spider shut the door, and walked back and sat down. The habit of obedience to Steadman was deeply ingrained in him so that it was almost impossible for him not to move when the coach said move.

"I thought about putting you on waivers," Steadman said in a quieter tone. "Maybe if I hadn't known about Gallagher, I would have. Maybe, hell, I *would* have. But I knew I couldn't, so I thought about you for a long time, after I got through cussing about losing Brad and probably a championship."

He swung about in the swivel chair and looked away from Spider out the window at the rolling fairways of the golf course. Then he swung back.

"I finally figured out a way we may still win the championship," he said. "It's a long shot and I don't think it's going to work, but if it doesn't work, we haven't got a prayer anyway."

"What's that got to do with me?" Spider asked.

"Everything," Steadman said and leaned forward, his leg going rapidly. "You got to carry your load, Leggett. If you've got the guts."

Spider stared at him in amazement, and suddenly Steadman smiled.

"Funny thing," he said. "I think any shrimp like you who would poke Brad in the head has to have the guts. Good luck, kid."

58

Chapter 6

THE conspiracy of silence against Spider lasted only one day, but that one day was long enough. He had heard about other players being given the silent treatment, and had thought that it would not be so bad. He was basically a loner, and he did not think that it would be disturbing if he did not have to indulge in small conversation with his teammates. Most of the time he could not think of much to talk about with them other than the game itself.

But he found quickly in the long meeting, practice, and the time in the locker room before and after, that there was an enormous difference in being quiet by preference and being regarded as if he did not exist. Not even Gangel, his closest friend on the club, would talk to him.

It started after he left Steadman's office and walked across the golf course to the dressing rooms. A few players were already there, some for whirlpool treatment for pulled muscles, others, the few who were always early because they liked to dress slowly and take particular care with ankle or knee bandages. Usually, when Spider entered the room, each of them would look up and greet him casually. This time, he might have been a ghost. No one looked at him or said anything to him.

He took his clothes off slowly, hanging the trousers and jacket carefully in his locker and went into the shower room, where he shaved his ankles and halfway up his calf, preparatory to taping. Gangel was in the room doing the same thing and Spider, without thinking, said "Hi, Dick. How's it going?"

Gangel paid studious attention to what he was doing and did not acknowledge Spider's greeting by so much as a flick of an eyebrow. Spider looked at him for a few moments, then shrugged and went about his business.

Back in the locker room, he suited up, leaving off his shoulder pads and jersey until after the meeting. In the meeting, it was not so bad since no one but the coaches talked anyway. He watched movies of the Green Bay defense with strict attention, studying particularly the moves of the All-Pro defensive back who would be working on him. He had never had much luck with Hap Aldridge, who was a big, very fast man with seven years experience and tremendously quick reactions. Watching him on the scouting film, Spider forgot his personal problems in trying to discover what, if any, Aldridge's weaknesses were.

He decided that if anything, Aldridge had a tendency to

play the receiver a little too tight, depending on his speed and reaction to save him on a deep pattern. Twice the Bears, the club the Packers had played the week before, tried a stop-and-go pattern on the defensive back. and once it seemed that the receiver had broken clear but Aldridge batted the ball away with a final, dazzling burst of speed.

He was curious about how Allie Berman, the little offensive coach, intended to attack Aldridge and the rest of the superb Packer pass defense. When the film had been run, Berman diagrammed the basic plays which would comprise the Ram ready list for the week, and Spider noted the slight changes in patterns and blocking assignments which made these plays different from what they had been the week before.

When Berman got to Aldridge in his brief resumé of the characteristics and tendencies of the Packer defensive backs, he looked straight at Spider, the first person outside of Steadman on the club who had done that all day.

"We'll try to make him deep conscious early," Berman said. "He plays a shallow defense, and he gets away with it because he's faster than most of the flankers he plays against and as fast as the rest. If Gallagher were healthy, we'd double-team him on deep patterns, sending Gallagher down behind him on one play and Leggett on the next and keeping that up until he ran out of gas. We could tire him out that way and then give Gallagher or Leggett a rest for two plays and send him deep with a pretty good chance of out-running Aldridge when he was tired and leg weary."

He turned to the blackboard and traced a deep sideline pattern for the flanker back, drawing the cut to the sideline at a sharp angle cutting slightly back toward the line of scrimmage.

"What we will try to do now," he said, "is impress him with the threat of the deep ball. We'll send the flanker deep on patterns for the first two or three series, and Brad—I mean, Frog—may even waste a play throwing deep to that side. If the receiver is open, fine, but I doubt that he will be open deep, early in the game. What we want to create in Aldridge is the fear and the idea that we are trying to get behind him."

He began to erase the blackboard, and there was a stirring of chairs as the offensive team began to get up, but he turned and stopped them.

"There's one more thing," he said slowly. "I know all of you must be shocked and disappointed that we will have to play without Brad Thomas for the rest of the season. We're putting Brad on injured reserve today, and we'll bring Pete Axthelm up from the taxi squad as number two quarterback. I won't pretend that the loss of Brad makes no difference. Obviously, it makes a big difference. But the coaches feel that Frog is more than good enough to carry this club. If we didn't feel that way, he wouldn't be here today. If you give Frog the effort and the dedication you have always given Brad, I think you will find that we'll keep on winning."

He stopped and scratched his head, and it seemed to Spider as if the assistant coach were looking directly at him again.

"The one thing we cannot afford," Berman went on, "the one thing that no professional football club can ever afford, is dissension and bitterness between players or between players and coaches. Whatever has happened here has happened, and is over with, and no animosity should be carried over to the future. One of the reasons this has been a good club is that there have been no personal feuds on it, no players who were soreheads or clubhouse lawyers, no player who wasn't a part of the club as a whole. With Brad out, we're going to have to depend even more on this kind of closeness. I hope all of you will think about that. That's all."

He waved a hand in dismissal, and the players closed their play books and began straggling back to the dressing room.

If Spider had some small hope that Berman's admonition would have an effect on the attitude of the other players toward him, he found out very soon that it did not.

He put on his shoulder pads and tightened the laces, then put his jersey on. Usually another player would automatically help pull the jersey down over the bulge of the pads in back, where it was difficult for the player, putting it on, to reach. This time, no one paid attention to Spider as he struggled to reach up from behind and find a piece of jersey so that he could pull it down over the pads. He wrestled with the problem for five minutes before he finally got the jersey on, and he was the last player to leave the dressing room for the practice field.

During the workout, no one addressed a remark to him. Frog seemed a little nervous as the play rehearsals began, but he settled down quickly, and he threw well, as he always had. He was a big, tall quarterback from Texas Christian University, standing six-seven and weighing 240, and Spider thought, wryly, that it was a good thing he had not taken a punch at Howard. If Thomas had knocked him out, Howard would probably have taken his head off.

Axthelm was a rookie from an Ivy League college, and he

suffered from a severe case of the jitters. Fresh from the taxi squad, he had worked mostly as the quarterback who impersonated the quarterback for the opponents during practice, and, although he was thoroughly familiar with the Ram offense, his voice had a deplorable tendency to slide up into a squeak when he tried to call signals for the veterans.

He threw the ball well, though, and after the first thirty minutes, he regained control of his voice and began to improve his play execution.

Even with Gallagher sidelined, though, the workout was less physically wearing than the one the day before. Another rookie from the taxi squad spelled him at flanker back, and most of the patterns called were the short squareouts with which Berman hoped to fool Aldridge on Sunday. Only rarely did Spider have to run a deep pattern, and he had plenty of rest between the long runs.

Usually the Los Angeles sports writers skipped the midweek practices, depending on Teale to brief them on what had happened, but on this afternoon, they had turned out in force to assess for themselves how well Howard would be able to substitute for Thomas.

They stood in a small knot on the sideline, watching the passes with super-critical eyes and questioning Jack Teale, the Ram publicity man, at some length. Spider was not aware of them until the practice had ended, and he was walking by himself back to the dressing room.

He looked up in surprise when a voice said, "Hello, Leggett."

"Hi," he said automatically, then recognized the owlish face of Jack Oslen, the *Times* columnist.

"Read my column the other day?" Oslen asked.

Spider nodded but did not say anything.

"What did you think about it?" Oslen insisted.

"It was good," Spider said. He looked ahead to the 1 of the team trying to see if any of them had noticed Os talking to him. None of them were looking back, but Spic was uncomfortable. He could imagine how they would fe if they saw the writer talking to him, and then he came ou with another column complaining about how little the Ran passers used him.

"You think it will help any?" Oslen asked.

"What do you mean?" Spider asked.

"You think they'll throw to you?"

"They throw to me," Spider said.

"Not enough," Oslen told him. "Sure, you had a little trouble earlier but who else they got? Especially now with Gallagher sick."

"I'm not complaining," Spider said apprehensively. They were about to enter the dressing room by now, and he did not want to go in with Oslen, so he stopped.

"Maybe Howard will throw to you more," Oslen said. "I always figured it was something personal between you and Thomas. Was that it?"

"No," Spider said shortly. "Excuse me. I have to get something out of my car."

He turned, and walked to his car, and waited until Oslen had disappeared into the dressing room before he started back. He waited outside for a few moments so that it would not seem as if he had been with the columnist, then walked in and tried to be inconspicuous as he made his way to his locker. He noticed that Oslen was talking to Frog Howard

and hoped, briefly, that the writer would devote his time and space to Howard and forget Spider Leggett.

He unlaced his low cuts and slipped them off, then sliced through the tape on his ankles and ripped it free in a quick motion. He was pleasantly tired, and often at the end of practice he enjoyed simply sitting in front of his locker and relaxing, listening to the conversations around him and relishing the tired relaxation which followed prolonged exercise. Gangel's locker was next to his and usually the two of them talked over the problems of the upcoming game but on this afternoon, Gangel went about undressing silently and quickly, self-consciously avoiding looking at Spider or talking to him.

The dressing room was quieter than normal on this day, and Spider could hear Oslen's voice as he talked to Howard at the other end of the room, although he could not hear what he said or what Howard answered. He stood up and started to peel his jersey off, but it caught under the pads in back, and he tugged hard to free it. The material was wet with perspiration and clung under the pads, and he finally pulled the jersey down and reached behind to try to free it.

He looked at Gangel to see if his friend had noticed his difficulty, but the tall, skinny end was ostentatiously absorbed in examining his shoes. Spider gritted his teeth and fumbled behind his back between his shoulder blades until he thought he had pulled the bulk of the jersey over the bottom edge of the pads. He crossed his arms in front, grasped the bottom of the jersey on each side, and pulled up again.

The stubborn jersey hung again on the pad, and he pulled hard, beginning to lose his temper. The shirt came loose suddenly and hung briefly under his chin, hurting his sore jaw

so that he emitted an involuntary grunt of pain as he pulled it over his head and stripped it from his arms.

"You're welcome," Oslen said from behind him. "I thought you were going to be stuck in there forever."

"Thanks," Spider said ungraciously. He sat down on his stool, trying to ignore Oslen and hoping that the other players would not feel that he had asked for this interview.

"What happened to your jaw?" Oslen asked, peering at Spider's face.

"Got an elbow last Sunday," Spider said. "Nothing much."

"I didn't notice it after the game," Oslen said. "When did it happen?"

"Late," Spider said. "I don't remember exactly."

"Knock you out?" Oslen asked, eyeing Spider closely.

"No," Spider said.

"Someone hang you on a clothesline?"

"Something like that," Spider said.

"Funny," Olsen said. "I don't remember you getting hurt. You have to leave the game?"

"It was on third down," Spider said. "Punting team came on, and I went off. By the time we went back on, I was OK."

"I talked to you right after the game," Oslen said. "Remember?"

"I guess so," Spider said.

"I didn't notice anything then," Oslen persisted. "The way it looks now, something should have showed."

"They don't swell for a long time," Spider said. "I had ice on it on the sideline. Doc controlled the swelling. He's good at that."

Oslen looked at him quizzically, then moved away to talk to the coaches. Spider heaved a deep sigh of relief and loosened the laces on his pads, then lifted them carefully over his head, trying to avoid touching the side of his jaw. Gangel looked at him as if he were going to say something, then glanced around the dressing room and turned away.

Spider stood for a long time under the shower, waiting for the rest of the players to finish, and dress, and get out of the locker room. When he had finished toweling and returned to his locker, nearly all had left. Only Skeeter Tilson, the big Negro fullback, was still there, fiddling with something in his locker.

Spider began to dress rapidly, not saying anything to Tilson, knowing Skeeter could not talk to him anyway.

So he was shocked to feel a hand on his shoulder as he was leaning over, one foot on the stool, lacng his shoes.

"Feel pretty bad, I guess," Tilson said softly.

"I'm all right," Spider said. He liked Tilson, a big, powerful man with a surprisingly gentle manner off the field. He was a great fullback.

"Look," Tilson said. "I can't take any of the load off your back, Spider. But remember one thing. It'll pass. For you, it's going to last a week, two weeks, three weeks at the most. All you have to do is gut it out, buddy."

"Gut it out," Spider said, suddenly angry at the players who had presumed to punish him. "All I got to do is gut it out for maybe three weeks. How would you like to have to do that?"

Tilson looked at him for a long moment, then grinned widely.

"You think about that a while, Spider," he said. "You think about it, and then you figure out how long I've been gutting it out."

Chapter 7

Spider spent a long night thinking about that, and when he had finished, his own problem had receded into the minor difficulty that he should have considered it from the beginning. He had never thought much about the problem of people such as Tilson and the other Negroes on the Ram squad. He knew that on some clubs in the league, there was a sharp division between black and white players, but there had never been such a division on the Rams, and he had not been really aware of the problem. He had always considered that in football—indeed, in all sports—players were judged on their ability alone, and the color of their skin was immaterial.

In the early hours of the morning, he started to call Tilson and apologize to him, but when he realized it was three o'clock, he did not. He knew he could not approach the big fullback in the dressing room, but he determined to tell him how he felt as soon as he could.

When Spider reached the locker room, no one paid any attention to him, but they would not have under any circumstances. Brad Thomas was out of the hospital, his right hand in a cast, and the players were gathered around him, trying to find out how he felt and how long it would be before he could play. Spider sneaked behind the group to his locker and began quietly to suit up.

He was ready to go to the team meeting before the group around Brad broke up and began going back to their lockers. Spider sat back and relaxed and gloried in the peace he had found during the night. He looked at the seven Negro players on the club and wondered why it had never occurred to him before that they might have special problems which extended beyond the dressing room and beyond the small life inside the Ram organization.

He looked at Thomas, who had his right arm in a sling. The quarterback was standing by Tiny Ross's locker, talking to his roommate and laughing. Spider was surprised that Thomas could be so cheerful in the face of adversity.

He felt no animosity toward Brad. The fight seemed a long time ago and the controversy not important. All Spider wanted to do was play well for the rest of the season, then begin afresh with a new team. He had made up his mind that he would not be as self-centered as he had been. The regimentation of playing with a unit and accepting the rules of the unit had galled him, but he understood that it was a part of the life of a professional football player. He thought again of Skeeter Tilson and the vastly more demanding and important problems that he had overcome in his advance to a meaningful position in life.

Wrapped up in his thoughts, he had not noticed Thomas coming across the dressing room toward him and he looked up only because the room had suddenly grown quiet, and he wondered why.

Thomas stopped in front of him and smiled.

"Hey, hard head," he said. "How your jaw?"

Spider stood up involuntarily and felt his face. He was shocked that Brad had talked to him, and he did not know how to reply, so he was silent.

"You got a concrete head," Brad said. "I'm sorry, Spider. I was riding you, and I had it coming. Let's forget it. Okay?"

He held out his left hand, and Spider took it without thinking and shook it. Thomas held up the cast.

"I learned my lesson," he said. "Never hit another Texan in the head."

Spider laughed, and a ripple of laughter ran through the dressing room; Spider looked around at the other players.

He looked back at Brad and tried to think of something to say.

"I'm sorry," he got out. "Look, I was out of line. I'm sorry."

"You were right," Brad said. "I was wrong. A quarterback can't afford patterns or habits or prejudices, Spider. You're a good receiver. I should have realized it and thrown to you until you got out of the slump. But my head's almost as hard as yours."

There did not seem to be much to say in answer to that, so Spider was silent. Brad slapped him on the shoulder and

71

turned away, and he went back to the stool and sat down again, dazed.

He thought for a little while that Thomas's apology would lift the ban on conversation with him but by the time he had finished the meeting and the practice, he discovered he was wrong. Although Thomas was pleasant to him, the other players still ignored him.

After the workout, he dressed in the usual silence, and he had decided that Tilson was right and the penance would continue for much longer. Brad did not talk to him as he dressed. Tilson, although he looked at him and winked once, said nothing.

He had showered and dressed in a hurry, and he was ready to leave while the rest of the club was still getting into street clothes. He started to walk out of the room, resigned to his lot, but as he reached the door, Thomas called out to him.

"Hold on a second, Spider," the veteran quarterback called. "I've got something to say, and I want you to hear it."

Spider stopped and waited. He was uncomfortable with the attention of the other players on him, and he hoped that what Thomas had to say would be quick.

"What I want to say is for the club, not just Spider," Brad said. "You all know what happened in here the other day, and you all know why it happened. No matter what you think, it was my fault. I've been with this team for seven years now and I am—or I should be—a mature football player. Spider has been here three years, and one of these years, he can give us a great season. He might have given us one this season—he may still give us one this season—if I hadn't been stubborn and unreasonable. I guess I started this year

72

resenting the fact that Lyman and Terry were gone, and I'd have to start all over again with new receivers. That sure as heck wasn't Spider's fault, and it wasn't Gangel's. We did all right for the first half, and I guess I thought I could make it without good receivers; I didn't have to take the time to adjust if someone dropped a pass or two."

He stopped and raised the cast up.

"I got this for being wrong, and I deserved it," he said quietly. "If I had been more concerned with Spider and less with my own frustrations, I wouldn't have asked for the shot he gave me, and if I had not been irritated because the passing wasn't going well, I wouldn't have hit Spider."

He stopped again and looked around at the players, very slowly.

"I know you've decided to give Spider the silent treatment," he said. "I can't stop that. I'm only a team captain. But if you're doing it because of what happened between me and Spider, then you better give me the silent treatment, too. Or better, give me the silent treatment and not Spider."

He looked at the cast ruefully and grinned.

"You're going to have to live with him on the field for the next six weeks," he said. "Not me. Think it over."

He nodded to Spider and walked across the room to him and said, "Come on, hard head. I need a ride home."

When they got in Spider's sports car, Spider realized that Brad had meant it when he said he needed a ride home. With the cast on his right hand, he could not drive.

"How did you get here?" he asked foolishly, not able to think of anything else to say.

"Doc brought me from the hospital," Brad said matter-of-factly. "They give you a hard time?"

"Not too hard," Spider said. "Nothing I can't handle."

Thomas looked at him thoughtfully as Spider backed the small car out of the parking slot and waited for a break in the traffic before driving out into the street.

"I meant what I said in there," he said. He tapped the cast on the dashboard. "When I get this thing off and start throwing again, you'll get your share."

Spider felt light with relief and happiness, and he laughed out loud.

"Hey," he said. "Don't throw as hard as you hit, man. I'd need a catcher's mitt to hold the ball."

"Just a lucky punch," Brad said, then grimaced. "Or unlucky, I should say."

"I'm sorry," Spider said sincerely. "I guess I lost my head, Brad."

"Forget it," Thomas said. "It's over, and there's nothing either one of us can do about it, Spider."

For the rest of the drive, they talked about the Ram offense and the problems for the game coming up, and Spider was surprised to find how much Thomas knew about the habits of the Green Bay defensive backs. The veteran quarterback knew their idiosyncrasies better than Spider, who had been studying little else for several days.

When he let Brad out in front of his apartment, he thanked him again for the speech he had made in the dressing room.

"Look," Thomas said. "That wasn't just for your benefit, Spider. It was for the club. One of the things you still have to learn, I think, is that as far as the Rams go, you are first a member of the organization. It's not easy to forget yourself and do what has to be done without thinking about whether you want to do it or not. When you can run your patterns,

74

Spider, and run them as one part of the whole, then you'll be a better receiver for it, and the Rams will be a better ball club for having you. You're a loner, I know, and that's okay when you're not operating as a player. But loners on the field are a handicap to everyone else. Think about that."

"Sure," Spider said. "I'll think about it."

Brad closed the car door and turned away, and Spider pulled the little sports car away from the curb slowly. He drove home thoughtfully, aware, finally, that it had not been from human kindness that Thomas had stood up for him to the rest of the club. He just doesn't want to lose any of that championship money, Spider thought. Or Super Bowl money.

With Howard running the team and Axthelm moving in as the number two quarterback, the practices did not go quite as smoothly as they usually did with Brad quarterbacking, but to Spider, they seemed to go well enough. Axthelm threw a soft ball, easy to catch, and although he lacked polish as a ball handler, he showed that he had the potential to play in the big league. The rest of the players were civil to Spider, but no more than that. In spite of Brad's remarks, they seemed to retain a good deal of their animosity to the player whose hot temper might have cost them a championship.

He and Gangel were soon back on a friendly footing, and Spider told himself that he did not need the good wishes of the other players. In the workouts, he ran his patterns as crisply as he could and drove himself savagely, determined to prove to himself, if no one else, that he was as good as any other member of the Ram team.

The patterns came easily to him now, and after the Wednesday practice, he asked Gangel if he wanted to stay out late and work on catching the ball. The tall receiver grinned and shook his head.

"Not me, buddy," he said. "By the time we get through with the regular work, I've had it."

"Okay," Spider said. "I read somewhere once that Raymond Berry used to stay out late and work on catching bad passes. If it helped him, maybe it would help me."

"I expect you got the right guy to throw you bad passes, when you asked me," Gangel told him. "But all I want right now is a hot shower and then a big steak."

He trotted away and Spider picked up the balls he had wheedled from Bill Granholme, the equipment manager, and started reluctantly to follow him. He had taken only a few steps when Frog Howard stopped him.

"You working with Granholme now?" the tall quarterback asked, motioning to the balls. "Or you going into the sporting goods business?"

His voice was friendly, and Spider grinned thinly.

"No," he said. "I just wanted to stay out and work on catching bad balls if I could get anyone to throw to me. Dick's too pooped."

"Catching bad balls?"

"Yeah," Spider said. "Low and behind, high and away, too far to one side or the other one. You don't see too many like that in a ball game, and if you don't know how to handle them without thinking, you drop them."

Howard was silent for a moment, regarding Spider thoughtfully.

"Who gave you that idea?" he asked.

"A story in *Sports Illustrated* about Raymond Berry,"

Spider said. "He used to stay out after practice with John Unitas, and they'd work on it."

"Okay," Frog said, sighing in mock resignation. "If it was good enough for Berry and Unitas, I guess I can do it, too. Gimme the balls."

"You mean you'll throw to me?" Spider asked in surprise.

"Sure," Frog said. "I got a strong arm. And it wouldn't do me any harm to get in a little extra practice either. Especially now."

Spider gave him the footballs, and the two players trotted down to the end of the practice field. There a frame had been rigged with a net so that balls missed by the receiver were caught by the net, which acted as a giant backstop and saved the time and effort needed in retrieving stray passes.

At the other end of the field, Rocky Stebbins, the rookie place kicker, was practicing with the help of Axthelm, who held the ball for him, and Rabbit Laguerre, who caught them and ran the ball back, cutting and faking as if he were in a broken field. None of them paid any attention to Frog and Spider.

"Tell me where you want it," Frog said. "You want to run a pattern?"

"Just the end of it," Spider said. "After the cut. Try a few low and behind me, if you can. That's the toughest ball for me to catch."

He made a quick cut, and accelerated, and looked for the ball and it came hard and low and just behind him so that he had to twist and bend to get his hands on it. He held the ball and straightened up, tucking it away at once. Berry had called the act of putting the ball in the crook of his arm putting it in the bank, and Berry did it automatically, even if he was only picking up a stray ball on the field. Spider had made himself do the same thing until it was a conditioned reflex.

"Nice catch," Frog called. "Was that about where you wanted it?"

"This time, make it a little lower and farther behind," Spider told him. "I'd like to work out just where it has to be before you can't get it."

They worked for half an hour and Spider found that the gangling Howard had a wonderful touch and extraordinary accuracy. No matter how he asked for the pass to be thrown, the ball arrived at the proper speed and at the right spot. He concentrated on the ball low and behind him for most of the time, but he worked on other special catches as well.

He practiced going down hard, stopping to spin, and crouch, and catch the ball off the ground, scooping it up with both hands and his forearms. He worked on diving catches and catches over his head, and the results were not as cheering as he had hoped they would be.

He quit, at last, on a successful diving catch and gathered up the footballs. As he joined Howard for the long walk to the dressing room, he shook his head sadly.

"I don't see how the devil Berry did it," he said. "I've watched him in the movies and he makes some of those catches look so easy. I try them, and I can't control the ball."

"I bet he couldn't either when he started," Howard said. "It takes time."

"I guess so," Spider said. "Thanks for working with me today, Frog."

"You not going to quit on one day?"

78

"No," Spider said. "But I can't expect you to stay out with me."

Howard held out his hand.

"You got a partner as long as you want," he said. "The extra work helps me, too. I'll aim for Johnny U and you aim for Berry."

Chapter 8

B**y** the time the Rams wound up preparation for the Green Bay game with the short Saturday morning drill devoted to loosening up and the final work for the special teams, Spider had regained his poise and looked forward eagerly to the game itself.

The extra work in the late afternoon with Howard had not yet noticeably improved his ability to catch balls thrown too wide, too low, too high or behind him, but he had developed a strong confidence in the ability of the Texas Christian graduate. Steadman had noticed their extracurricular efforts on the second afternoon they stayed out late and had asked Howard if the extra work didn't tire his arm, but Howard denied that it did.

81

"Don't overdo it," Steadman said. "If it feels stiff, quit."

He said nothing to Spider so the young receiver decided that Steadman was not very much worked up about his overdoing it. He grinned at Howard as the coach walked away.

"Maybe I better get Axthelm to work with me," he said. "I'm in enough trouble hitting Brad on the hand with my head. You come up with a sore arm working with me overtime, and they'll lynch me."

Frog laughed and flexed his right arm. Despite his exceptional height, his arms were thick and well-muscled, and to the wiry Leggett, they looked as sturdy as manila cable.

"Never had a sore arm in my life," Frog said. "Coach one time told me I never would with my motion. I get a lot of wrist in my throw, and it takes the pressure off the elbow."

Spider had seen Howard casually snap a pass sixty yards in the air with almost no effort, and he had wondered how far the big man could throw the ball if he put his weight into it. He asked, and Howard shook his head.

"I got no idea," he said. "What's more, I don't intend to try to find out. I throw it as far as I have to, and I guess a few times in ball games I've thrown it as far as I could, but no one ever measured it."

They had gone back to their special practice then, and Steadman had made no further effort to slow them down. Dickey, the end coach, was delighted and gave Spider specific problems to work on and some suggestions on catching difficult passes.

"Don't expect to get the ball into your hands every time," he said once after watching Spider for a while. "Sometimes if you can get a finger tip on the ball, you can flip it up and then catch it. Try to slow it down, then grab it."

82

Spider worked on that and found it as difficult as the other techniques of catching bad balls. During the regular practice, though, he found the well thrown balls, which were the rule with Howard, much easier to handle. He asked Dickey about that, and the end coach grinned at him.

"They aren't any easier to catch," he said. "You just think they are. As long as you think they are, then you've got more confidence, and you'll catch more balls. I hope."

After the short Saturday morning practice, Spider went back to his apartment and watched a college football game on television, with Gangel. He felt curiously at peace, and he watched the college players with professional detachment, paying particular attention to the receivers and the defensive backs and deciding that if he were playing college ball now, with all that he had learned since becoming a pro, he would probably catch a hundred balls a year.

"You want to go to a movie?" Dick asked when the game was over.

"Not me," Spider said. "I'm going to eat and go over my play book a couple of times and go to sleep. We got a big one tomorrow, Dick."

"I guess you're right," Gangel said. He got up and stretched. "But I'm too nervous to do that. I think I'll catch a movie before I go to bed."

"See you at the hotel," Spider said. "Take it easy."

The Rams spent the night before a home game in a hotel. They had dinner together there, and then they were on their own until the eleven o'clock curfew. Steadman felt that the custom gave the married players a peaceful night away from wives and children and made sure that the single ones got a good night's rest before the game.

Spider, who had been restless and almost sleepless on the nights before previous games, slept easily and well on this Saturday night and awakened refreshed and anxious for the game to start.

The day was bright and clear and not too warm. On the way to the Coliseum, Spider, who had taken his own car instead of riding in the bus, commented on the weather.

"Glad it's cool," he said. "I hate it when it's about a hundred on the field. No way to keep your hands dry."

"Me, I don't sweat much," Gangel said. "I don't know why."

"I don't usually," Spider said. "But a couple of times, the Coliseum has been a real pressure cooker."

But it was pleasantly cool and crisp as he went through the calisthenics before the game, enjoying the feeling of loosening up. The big cement bowl was filling early; the game with the Packers was always a sellout and on this Sunday, with the Rams leading in the race for the Coastal Division championship and the Packers ahead in the Central Division, the demand for tickets had been tremendous.

At the other end of the field, the Green Bay club was going through its own set of calisthenics, and Spider tried to pick out Aldridge, the big defensive back who would be on him during the game. He finally found the green shirt with the big white 24 on it and briefly watched Aldridge doing calisthenics. Even at the far end of the field, he looked tall and rangy, and Spider knew that he would be giving away four inches in height and more than that in reach. His big advantage over Aldridge would be in speed, and he was actually only two or three tenths of a second faster than the Packer back, over a hundred yards.

He was not sure how much faster he would be on short spurts, but he knew he accelerated much quicker than most pro players, primarily because he was so much smaller than the others.

When the club left the field to go back to the dressing room and put on pads preparatory to the start of the game, he trotted beside Frog. The big quarterback moved easily, and it seemed to Spider that he had to take two steps to one for Howard.

"How do you feel?" Spider asked him.

"Good," Frog said. "I got butterflies in my belly, but I feel pretty good. It's a lot different knowing you're going to start, and it's all up to you."

"You can do it," Spider said confidently.

"I hope so," Frog said. "Boy, I hope so."

Spider put his pads on quickly and sat in the little cubicle he shared with Gangel with his legs out and his head leaning back against the wall, trying to relax. He thought of his body muscle by muscle, starting at his feet, consciously trying to relax each one, draining the tension from his body.

Just before they went out on the field, Steadman gathered them in the big room where he would later hold his press conference.

"This is a big game," he said, quietly. His voice was unemotional, and he made no effort to arouse them. "It will— or it could—show a lot about how we will do the rest of the year. If you have confidence in yourselves and play your ball game, I think you will win. The Packers will be coming hard when we have the ball because they'll want to put pressure on Frog. We know he can take the pressure. If we can handle their blitz, or keep them out of the pocket, Frog should be able to hurt them throwing the ball. That's all."

They left the dressing room quietly and walked down the long ramp to the opening on to the field, where they stopped. The Rams had won the toss, and the offensive team would be introduced and Spider, in spite of the calm and confidence he had felt earlier, felt his stomach flutter. Out in the bright sunlight, the Ram band and the girls who made up the cheerleader corps had formed a long double line leading toward the goalposts. When his name was called, he would run between the lines, through the goalposts and out to the center of the field. In the past, he had known the sound of boos on the short journey; this time he did not know what to expect, but he hoped that the boos, if any, would be quiet.

The public address system boomed—"At spread end, number 81, Spider Leggett!" and one of the TV people tapped him on the shoulder and Spider sprinted out into the sunshine. Some players had told him that they were not aware of the noise of the crowd when they were introduced, but Spider had always heard either the applause or the boos. Now there was an enthusiastic silence, broken by scattered boos as he ran to midfield and Jack DeFord, the big left tackle who had been introduced before him, offered him his hand.

The excitement of the game had begun to take hold of Spider now, and he danced about impatiently waiting for the rest of the offensive team to be introduced. He greeted them noisily as they came on the field; most of them returned his greeting stolidly, their faces preoccupied. Howard grinned

86

at him tightly, his face tense and drawn now with the responsibility of carrying the club.

On the kickoff, Spider stood tensely on the sideline and watched as Rabbit Laguerre fielded the ball five yards deep in the end zone and rashly decided to run it out. He reached the 12-yard line before the Packers buried him in an avalanche of tacklers. Spider was surprised to see Laguerre hop nimbly to his feet and run to the sideline. He had half expected to see the back mashed out of shape at the bottom of the mountain of green jerseys.

In the huddle, Howard knelt on one knee and snapped the signal out very quickly, so that Ottum, the big running back, held up a hand. "Once more, Frog," he said. "Slow it down, baby."

Howard called the play again. It was a drive over the tackle with Tilson carrying the ball, and the big Negro fullback churned four yards before the Packer linebackers knocked him down.

Again Howard called a running play and this time Ottum, sweeping wide to his left, was trapped behind the line of scrimmage when the Green Bay middle linebacker ignored the fake into the line and went with the ball.

It was third and 8 when the Ram huddle formed, and Howard hesitated a moment. The team was on its own 14-yard line, and Spider wondered whether Frog had enough confidence in himself to call a pass in such dangerous territory. The call would have been an easy one for Thomas. The first string Ram quarterback never called a play with the idea that it would fail.

Howard barked the signal, and it was a sideline pass to Spider. With two running plays called before, Spider had had no chance to run deep fakes on Aldridge, and the Green Bay defensive back was notorious for playing receivers close, so Spider had little hope of getting free on this call. Aldridge would be looking for the sideline just deep enough for a first down.

Spider hesitated a moment coming out of the huddle and whispered to Frog.

"If's he's up tight, square out and go," he said, hoping that Frog would realize that if Aldridge was up close on him when he cut to the sideline, he would fake the cut and go deep. It would be no use to run out the original pattern if it were covered; if the square out and go worked, it could mean a long gain.

Howard looked at him blankly, and Spider set himself to wait for the snap signal, uncertain if the quarterback had understood him or not. He looked up at Aldridge across the line of scrimmage and the Green Bay back had cheated up even closer to the line than usual. He stared back at Spider impassively, dark face intent and calculating.

At the snap of the ball, Spider came out of his three point stance with a sprinter's explosive start and drove directly at Aldridge, who gave ground, grudgingly.

Spider took a short jab step to his right, then cut back hard to the left toward the sideline, and Aldridge was on top of him. The big halfback sliced in between Spider and the line of scrimmage, and Spider cut back to his right, racing up the sideline. As he made the move, he prayed that Frog had read him as they broke the huddle. If he threw to where Spider would have been on the sideline, the ball would be in the hands of Aldridge.

He was in the open now, the weak side safety angling over

toward him, and he looked back over his right shoulder. The ball hung high in the air on its trajectory toward him, and he forgot everything as he put on a burst of speed to reach it. As it came down, he jumped, and stretched, and tipped it in the air, then ran under it and grabbed it in his hands. He tucked it away, then looked for the weak side safety.

He was surprised to see that the safety was still yards away; it had seemed as if the jump and catch had taken minutes, but they must have taken place in a split second. He had the ball safely put away and his body under control, and he felt as if he were moving in slow motion as he gave the safety a strong head fake and cut to the middle of the field.

As he cut across the field, the strong safety, who had gone with Slats Shrake, the tight end, recovered and came across with a good angle on him but Gangel cut him down, and suddenly Spider was alone. The rest of the run was easy. He knew no one on the Packer club could run him down from behind.

He crossed into the end zone and jumped high in the air, then threw the football into the end zone. As he came down, Gangel grabbed him in a bear hug and danced him around, yelling incomprehensibly in his ear. The roar of the crowd beat down on him, and he shouted happily as he started for the sideline.

At the sideline, Howard was waiting for him, a broad grin splitting his face. He enveloped Spider's hand in his huge paw and slapped him on the shoulder.

"Great move," he hollered. "Great catch."

"I'm glad you read me," Spider said. "If you hadn't been on the ball, it could have been six the other way."

"I saw Aldridge cheat up when I started the count," Frog said. "I was kind of in a daze until then, but when I noticed him coming in too tight, I knew what you meant. It was a piece of cake after that."

Spider unsnapped his chin strap and walked over to the bench and sat down. As he wiped his face with a towel given him by one of Granholme's helpers, Al Berman, the offensive coach, squatted beside him.

"What was that pattern?" he asked, puzzled. "I thought it was a square out."

"It was," Frog said. He had seated himself at the small table with the phone to the scouts in the press box, near Spider. "We figured that if Aldridge played it too tight, we'd improvise. Or Spider figured it."

"I see," Berman said. "Suppose you hadn't read Spider's move or they had blitzed, and you hadn't had time to throw long?"

"They blitzed from the other side," Frog said. "You probably couldn't see the linebacker come. I had to throw early."

Berman was silent for a moment and Frog talked to the scout in the press box. When he had finished, Berman stood up.

"Well," he said, doubtfully. "It worked. You can't argue with that."

On the next Ram offensive series, Aldridge played deeper, conceding the short pass and cutting off the deep one. Once or twice during the rest of the game, Howard called deep plays to Spider, but Aldridge stayed close, and Howard went to another receiver.

After the 86-yard touchdown pass, the game settled down into a grim, bitter struggle, and the gains came hard and short. Often, with Aldridge playing back, Frog went to Spider on short yardage plays, and time and again Spider caught the ball on quick slants or sidelines, picking up first downs or key yardage.

But the Packer defense, near the Green Bay goal line, closed off the short passes, too, and when the game was over, Green Bay had won, 13-10, on a touchdown and two field goals, to the Rams' touchdown and field goal.

In the dressing room, Spider slumped disconsolately before his locker, his uniform wet with perspiration. Across the cubicle, Gangel sat with his hands on his knees and his head down. He and Spider had played every minute of offensive football, and both of them were exhausted.

Finally Gangel looked up and essayed a small smile.

"Anyway, you came out of the slump," he said. "How many balls did you catch?"

"I don't know," Spider said, honestly. "Doesn't make much difference. We lost."

Chapter 9

Spider had taken off his cleats and sliced the tape from his ankles, when there was a knock on the door of the cubicle. He looked up in surprise, because the writers usually did not get around to interviewing him until they had talked to the coaches and the stars. Must be Doc, he thought. The Ram team doctor checked on all the players after the game, whether they had been shaken up during play or not.

"Come in," Gangel said, raising his eyebrows at Spider.

A short, rather chunky man with dark hair and a lively, inquisitive face came in and smiled at them, his eyes disappearing into slits in the smile.

"Hi, fellas," he said, and held his hand out first to Spider, then to Dick. "Tough luck. You ought to have had that one."

93

"Thanks, Mal," Gangel said. "You can't make any mistakes against the Pack. They kill you."

"Can I use that?" Mal Florence said, laughing. "Seems like I have heard it before. Once or twice."

"Hi," Spider said. "Sure you didn't write it?"

"Many times," Florence said. He was the writer for the *Times* assigned to day-by-day coverage of the club, and most of the players liked him. He was fair and accurate. His criticisms stung more because of that, and he had, during the first half of the season, pointed out Spider's deficiencies dispassionately and by Spider's reckoning, too often.

"Good game," Florence said to Spider now. "How many balls did you catch?"

"I don't know," Spider said. "I didn't keep count."

"I got it here," Mal said. He took a sheaf of folded mimeographed paper out of his inner coat pocket and shuffled through it until he came to a page of statistics. "Let's see. Leggett—passes caught, ten. Yards gained, a hundred fifty-six. Touchdowns, one. How about that?"

"Hey," Gangel said, and whistled. "How about me?"

Florence consulted the statistics again.

"Four for sixty-seven yards, no touchdowns," he said. "Not bad for a rook, Dick."

"I'll take it," Dick said.

He had stripped, and he threw a towel over his shoulder.

"You want to talk to me about anything?"

"Not right now," Mal said. "I was looking for mighty mouse, here."

"Be good to him," Gangel said, smiling. "We may need him to make it to Super Bowl."

94

"I'll try," Florence said. When Gangel had left, he turned to Spider, his rather round face serious and intent.

"Why did Howard throw to you so much when Brad had *quit* throwing to you?" he asked.

Spider looked at him in consternation, not sure what he should say. To explain why Frog went to him in a tight situation and why Brad had not, he would have to explain all the problems he had had in this season, and he knew he could not do that.

"Our game plan was set up for Frog to throw more to me," he said lamely. "I mean, that's the way it worked out."

Florence made a quick note, then looked up at Spider, his eyes squinting shrewdly.

"I see," he said. "The best defensive back on the Packers is Aldridge, and the one guy that hasn't been catching passes for the Rams is Spider Leggett, so the last thing that the Packers would expect is for the Rams to throw to Leggett in Aldridge territory. That it?"

In spite of himself, Spider had to smile.

"More or less," he said.

"Come on," Mal said. "Look, Spider. I don't know you very well, and I can't say that all I want to do is see that you get a fair shake on this club, but I know as well as anyone who has been watching the Rams this year, that Brad quit throwing to you after the first couple of games. Now, all at once, Frog throws you twelve balls, and you catch ten, one for a long touchdown. The only thing that has changed on the Rams is the quarterback. How do you explain that?"

"I don't," Spider said. "I'm not the guy who makes explanations. The coaches do that. If they want to throw me the ball, I'll catch. If they don't throw it my way, I can't catch it."

Florence pondered for a moment, the chubby face intent.

"Would you say this is the best game you have played for the Rams?" he asked at last.

Spider thought about that for a while. He had never caught as many passes in one game for as many yards, and he had never caught more than one touchdown pass in a game, so obviously this was the best game he had played.

"Yes," he said. "It was the best game for me as an individual. There have been other games in which I had more satisfaction, because we won. No game, no matter what your personal statistics are, is a really good game if the club loses. The other club—maybe that was true today—the other club may be giving me the good day to cut off something else, so they can beat us."

"What did they cut off by giving you a good day?"

"I don't know," Spider said. "I don't even know if they were cutting off anything. Early in the season, I got double coverage, but I haven't had that in about six weeks, so I didn't expect it today. Green Bay cuts off almost everything all the time."

"Do you think you would have caught as many balls if Brad had been the quarterback instead of Frog?"

"No," Spider said, without thinking.

"Why not?"

"I take that back," Spider said. "Maybe with this game plan I would have. I don't know."

"Would you rather have Frog or Brad at quarterback?"

Spider looked at Florence for a long time before replying.

"No way I can answer that right, is there?" he said at last. "So I'm not going to answer it."

Florence shrugged and closed his notebook.

"Anyway, good luck," he said. "If Frog keeps throwing to you, the Rams could go all the way even without Thomas."

"I hope so," Spider said. "I sure hope so."

Florence left, and Spider finished undressing. He was surprised at how tired he was until he realized that his part in this game had been a far more violent one than he was accustomed to. When you catch ten balls, you get hit a lot more, he thought. Ten balls. How about that?

He had showered and was just finishing dressing when Oslen, the *Times* columnist, came in.

"You must feel good today," he said, peering owlishly at Spider through the horn rimmed glasses.

"Tired," Spider said. He was tired, and he felt a little light-headed from the release of tension. "I was pretty busy out there."

"You certainly were," Oslen said, warmly. "It's about time they started throwing to you. I guess Howard appreciates you more than Thomas did."

Spider said nothing to that. He adjusted the knot in his tie and slipped on his jacket.

"Was there any trouble between you and Thomas?"

"Trouble?" Spider said, trying to look surprised.

"I mean, how did you get along?"

"Real well," Spider said. "Brad and I are good friends."

"Why didn't he throw to you?"

"He threw to me," Spider said. "I told you that the other day."

"Not ten times in one game," Oslen said.

"Maybe I wasn't open ten times," Spider said.

"You were open. I saw the games."

"Look," Spider said irritably. "No matter what you saw, there wasn't any trouble between Brad and me. Frog threw to me ten times because the Green Bay defense covered me one-on-one, and I was the open man. Brad would have done the same thing."

"I don't think so," Oslen said. "Every defense in the league has taken you one-on-one since the third game of the season, Spider. I think the best thing that ever happened to you was when Thomas slipped and fell in the shower. If that is what really happened."

"What do you think happened?"

"I don't know," Oslen said, thoughtfully. "But I'm going to do my best to find out."

He nodded to Spider and left, and Spider watched him go with relief. As he walked out of the littered dressing room, Frog joined him, his face glum.

"I thought we might do it for a while," he said. "I still think we have a better club than Green Bay."

"We're still all right," Spider said. "We're a game ahead in our division with five to go, and the Colts have to play Green Bay yet. In Green Bay. The Packers can't do anything but help us until we meet them in the division playoff, Frog."

"That's right," Frog said, his face brightening. "And next time will be a different story, Spider."

"I think you're right," Spider said. They walked together up the long slant of the ramp toward the player parking area just outside the Coliseum and stopped when they reached Spider's car.

"How about the extra work?" Spider asked anxiously. "You still feel like doing it?"

"Sure," Frog said. "I think it helped out there today, Spider. I knew more about your moves, and I could anticipate better. Like on the bomb. I led you a little too much, but on what was really a broken pattern, it was a pretty good pass."

"It was a heck of a pass," Spider said. "You know, maybe we could work on something like that. Maybe there's some way I can show you if I'm being doubled or running into zone coverage right away and change the pattern. What do you think?"

"I think before we get into anything like that, we better take it up with Berman," Frog said. "He doesn't take very kindly to people inventing patterns without letting him know about it."

Spider laughed. The sting of the defeat had begun to die out, and he was anxious to get back to work with Frog on the patterns that had worked so well against Green Bay.

"I didn't mean we ought to put in our own private patterns," Spider said. "Just work out our own variations."

"That I'll buy," Frog said. He stuck out his hand. "Shake on it, ol' buddy."

Spider shook his hand, and Frog turned and walked away with the long loping stride which moved him with surprising speed. Spider watched the tall, ungainly-looking figure for a few moments, then got in his car.

"Looks like you two are real buddies," Oslen said from ten feet away, where he was sitting in his car. "I didn't know that."

"We're friends," Spider said shortly. He started the sports

99

car and raced the motor, drowning out something that Oslen was saying. He waved to the columnist and backed out and drove away, not wanting to talk to him any more.

As he made his way to the freeway and started to drive back to Long Beach, he switched on the car radio and listened to music. He was pleasantly tired, and he could feel the beginnings of aches and bruises which would be sore and stiff by the next day, but for the first time in a long time, he felt a sense of accomplishment. He had caught the ball well, and he had made a big contribution to the Ram offense. In spite of himself, he could not help hoping that Thomas's injury might keep him out of play for the rest of the year.

He banished the thought as soon as it had entered his mind and felt a strong sense of guilt that he would place his own well-being over the good of the team. For the rest of the ride to Long Beach, he concentrated on the music and did his best to forget his problems with the Rams. Most of them seemed to have dissolved in the last week, anyway.

For dinner, Spider went to a steak house not far from his apartment, a restaurant which he used often because the food was good and plentiful, and the prices were something less than the good restaurants in Los Angeles. He ate alone; sometimes Gangel joined him if his wife went to her mother's, but the young receiver had not offered to accompany him on this evening.

He was pleasantly surprised to find that, on one afternoon's play, he had assumed some of the status of a celebrity. Although the restaurant owner and most of the employees knew he played with the Rams, they had paid little atten-

100

tion to him on his previous visits. Now the manager made a point of coming over to him and shaking his hand.

"Tough one to lose, Spider," he said. "But they finally got around to using you the way they should have all along. You had a heck of a day."

"Thanks," Spider said. "I was lucky."

Several other people stopped to talk to him, most of them saying the same things that the restaurant manager had said. Spider found himself enjoying the unusual recognition thoroughly.

After he had finished dinner, he walked into the small bar and the manager said, "How about a drink?"

"Maybe a beer," Spider said. "I don't drink during the season. I don't drink much during the off-season, for that matter."

"Okay, a beer then," the manager said. He was a big, jovial man, an Italian whose name Spider could never remember. He felt a mild embarrassment now trying to think of the man's name.

He drank the glass of beer slowly, enjoying the cold bitterness on his tongue and listening to the manager give him his version of what the Rams could have done to beat Green Bay. It was amazing how much better most people could have done than the quarterback in any game the Rams lost.

"If Thomas had been in there," the manager wound up, "you can bet your bottom dollar the Rams wouldn't have lost. Don't you think so?"

"I thought Frog called a good game," Spider said quietly. "Of course Brad's the All-Pro and the best in the business, and everyone knows it, but I don't know if he could have done any better than Frog did today."

"Maybe not," the manager said. "I like both of them, anyway."

"So do I," Spider said. Many of the Rams came in this restaurant during the season, for the same reasons Spider did. "I just hope Frog stays healthy."

"He likes you," the manager said, slapping Spider on the back. "You're his favorite target, Spider."

Another man at the bar looked up and smiled. He looked vaguely familiar to Spider, so Spider nodded to him.

"That was the trouble with Thomas," the man said, nodding wisely. "He wouldn't throw to Spider here."

"You know Ozzie," the manager said.

"Sure," Spider nodded. "How are you?"

"Fine," Ozzie said. "I couldn't help hearing you say how Brad couldn't have called the game as good as Frog did today, and I agree with you. I've always figured Frog was a better quarterback."

"I didn't say that," Spider said hastily. He looked at his wrist watch ostentatiously and got up. "I got to go now," he said. All at once he remembered the manager's name. Antonio Triolo, like the big Ram defensive end. "Thanks, Tony," he said. "See you next week, maybe."

Chapter 10

Spider slept late the next morning, and when he awakened, he moved gingerly into the small kitchen to cook breakfast for himself. On Monday mornings, with all the small aches and pains left over from the Sunday game, he usually preferred to make his own breakfast, postponing the physical activity of showering, and dressing, and going out as long as possible.

As he fried bacon and scrambled eggs and put a pot of coffee on the stove, he took mental note of the sore spots. None of them, to his relief, seemed serious. There was a wide bluish-green bruise over his ribs where Aldridge had hung him with an elbow as he went by on one pass and various sore spots on his arms and legs, but he could move well enough and that was all that mattered.

He walked out to get the newspaper, for the first time in weeks anticipating reading it instead of dreading what the writers would have to say about him and dreading even more that they would say nothing at all.

Florence had written the game story in the *Times*, and Spider spread the paper out on the breakfast table to read as he ate.

"The Los Angeles Rams lost a battle with Green Bay Sunday," Florence had written. "but they may have won a war. For the first time this season, Coach John Steadman's team attacked with all its weapons and attacked well. That they lost is understandable, since they played for the first time in a long time without Brad Thomas throwing and directing the game. But Frog Howard demonstrated unusual poise and a wide-ranging appreciation of the Ram arsenal. He found one of the neglected items in the arsenal of extraordinary use against Green Bay. That would be Spider Leggett, the mini-receiver."

The rest of the story dealt in detail with the happenings in the game and Florence paid strong tribute to the catches Spider had made. He spent much of his story detailing the long touchdown pass and explaining that it had been a spur of the moment play set up by Spider. He had gotten his information from Frog, whose comments on Spider's play, as related by Florence, were almost fulsome in their praise.

"No one can seriously say that a team is benefited by the loss of a player of the stature of Brad Thomas," Florence wound up. "But in this case, it might be salutary for the Rams to operate for a few weeks under a fresh mind. Maybe

Brad had grown too set. Maybe the rest of the league was reading him too easily. Certainly the rest of the league had decided that he would not throw to Spider Leggett. Well, no one can disregard Spider in their game preparations after today."

Spider had finished the eggs and bacon, and he poured himself another cup of coffee. The coffee was not very good, but on this morning it tasted like nectar to him. He turned to Oslen's column, apprehensively.

"Mystery on the Rams" the head read.

Spider stirred the coffee, and sipped it, and burned his lips, He was reluctant to go on reading the column, but he could not curb his curiosity.

"On the surface," Oslen had written, "the Rams, despite their narrow loss to the Green Bay Packers in the Coliseum, have reason to be joyful today. All those who felt that this club would collapse in a heap if Brad Thomas were injured, found out that the club played even better with him on the sidelines and Frog Howard in the pilot's seat.

"Howard called a brilliant game against Green Bay. For the first time this year, the Rams were a total team on offense, with Howard calling in equal and thoughtful measure on the various weapons at his disposal. Of course, the major difference in this performance and Ram performances on previous Sundays, was the use of Spider Leggett in the offensive plan.

"Leggett demonstrated rather clearly that he has become one of the great receivers in the league. Many people thought that he would never achieve real stardom because of his size, but those people must have forgotten the heroics of another little man named Tommy McDonald. Tommy, with the Philadelphia Eagles, the Rams, and the Dallas Cowboys, proved a long time ago that a little man with courage, and good hands, and determination can be as good as anyone. Spider has all of that, plus more speed than Tommy had.

"He made one of the best catches this writer has ever seen on the long touchdown pass that Frog threw him early in the game. The ball was overthrown, but Leggett went high, tipped it with one hand, then ran under it and caught it. Not only did he catch the ball, but he retained enough poise and body control to fake the defender and score."

Spider drank his coffee happily. It had cooled as he read avidly, and he judged that it tasted better than most of the coffee he made.

"Watching Leggett's magnificent game Sunday," Oslen went on, "makes you wonder why Thomas refused to throw to him. True, Leggett dropped a few passes early in the season, but I submit that even receivers like Fears and Hirsch, at their peaks with the Rams, dropped balls now and then.

"The difference was that Van Brocklin and Waterfield kept throwing to Fears and Hirsch. Thomas quit on Leggett, and obviously he quit too soon. The little spread end has a genius for getting open, and he has hands and moves the equal of any in the league. The man he was beating Sunday, in case you may not have noticed, was Hop Aldridge, who was an All-Pro defensive back last season and for several years before that. He was not taking advantage of a rookie or beating a patsy. He was catching passes on one of the wiliest, quickest and best defensive halfbacks in football."

Spider took another drink of the coffee, which had become almost cold by now, but he did not notice. He had not realized what a job he had done the day before, he thought. I'm not that good, but maybe I'm better than some people think.

"Given a receiver of Leggett's clear-cut ability," Oslen wrote, "and a quarterback of Thomas's proven intelligence, you must wonder why Thomas saw fit to leave Leggett out of his plans in previous games. Certainly in the last month, the Ram pass offense has suffered from the paucity of targets Thomas used in his air attack. Why would he overlook Leggett? In practice, Leggett was catching the ball well and running his pattern better than the other Ram receivers.

"Behind Thomas's refusal to use him in game plans must lie something else. Both Thomas and Leggett deny that there has been any personal animosity between them. Yet there are a few clues for the watchful observer which might indicate otherwise."

Here it comes, Spider thought. He tried to remember what he had said to Oslen in the dressing room after the game, and he could not remember anything which might have given the writer an inkling that he had fought with the quarterback.

"The Ram publicity department put out a release saying that Thomas broke a knuckle on his right hand when he slipped and fell in the tile shower room at the Ram's Long Beach training camp," the story continued. "At first blush, that seems reasonable enough. But stop and think about it for a while. Most of us, at one time or another, have slipped on a bar of soap and taken a fall in the bath tub or in a shower. But most of us came out of it with a sprained wrist or a banged knee or at the worst, maybe a cracked tail bone.

"I checked with the accident department of a major insurance company to discover what percentage of broken knuckles they get from accidents like the one that Thomas was supposed to have had. This is a company which handles and processes literally thousands and thousands of claims a year for personal injury accidents. And the doctor I talked to told me that not in his entire experience, covering more than twenty years, had he had a claim for a broken knuckle suffered in a fall in a shower.

"The first reaction is to put your hand out to protect yourself, with the fingers spread and the hand palm down. In this position, it is very difficult to break a bone in the hand between the knuckle and the wrist. But that is where Thomas's injury happened, according to the Ram team doctor.

"The insurance doctor also said that a bone fracture from the knuckle to the wrist usually is the result of either something falling on the back of the hand and breaking one of the bones there, or—and mark this—of the clenched fist being driven into a hard surface with enough force to buckle the bone in the back of the hand."

Spider felt the small lump left on the side of his jaw and scowled. His jaw, he supposed, qualified as a hard, flat surface.

"The other day, Leggett came to practice with a lump on the side of his jaw," Oslen's column went on. "He said that he had caught an elbow during the game the week before, but any blow which could have left the bruise he had would certainly have knocked him down and probably would have knocked him out. We watched movies of that game, and Spider wasn't staggered. If he was hit by an elbow, he takes a punch better than most heavyweight fighters.

"Add the two things together, and you come up with something. Thomas broke his hand on a hard surface, and Leggett

108

has a sore jaw. From here, it looks like maybe a fight. If it was, Leggett lost in one way, but he won in another. He can play with a sore jaw and Thomas can't with a broken hand, and it certainly looks like Frog Howard is a better playmate for Leggett than Thomas was.

"Yesterday evening, after the game, Frog and Spider walked out of the dressing room together and they looked like old friends. Or maybe they are new friends. At any rate, they are better friends than Spider and Brad Thomas ever were."

Spider put the paper down and shook his head. Nothing Oslen had written could be challenged as to fact, but the picture he had painted of the feeling on the Ram club was certainly off. And the intimation was that Leggett and Howard were conspiring to make Brad look bad.

He glanced through the rest of the sports page, reading the stories of the other games in the two pro leagues. He found it difficult to keep his mind on what he was reading. The new problems that Oslen's column could create for him intruded on the written page, and finally he put the paper down.

He put the dirty dishes in the sink and, as usual, decided that he would wash them later. As he turned away, the telephone rang, and he went into the living room to answer it.

"Hey, star," Gangel's voice said. "You read the paper?"

"I read it," Spider said. "Oslen really helped a lot, didn't he?"

"Oslen?"

"Sure. In the *Times*."

"I mean the Long Beach paper," Gangel said. "You haven't read that yet?"

109

"No," Spider said. "What about it?"

"You sound like the greatest thing since sliced bread," Gangel said. "But Ozzie Tower has a column you might be interested in, too."

"I don't read the Long Beach paper," Spider said. "Not often. What does it say?"

"Read it," Gangel said. Spider started to say something else, but the phone went dead, and he realized that Gangel had hung up.

He looked at the phone for a moment, then placed the instrument in its cradle. He could not imagine what Tower could say that would mean much to him. He had a vague recollection of having met the Long Beach columnist, but he could not remember what he looked like, and he knew that he had never been interviewed by him. He decided that he would walk down to the drug store three blocks away and pick up the Long Beach paper.

It could not be worse than Oslen, he thought as he left the apartment. The morning was bright and crisp, and he enjoyed the clean, clear air. He liked living in Long Beach. The air was usually much cleaner than the smog-ridden atmosphere of Los Angeles, and he thought that Steadman had been wise to take the club out of the city for training.

He bought the Long Beach paper, and the other Los Angeles paper, and resisted the temptation to read them at the drug store. On the walk back to his apartment, he tried to forget about the game and about the papers, but he found himself hurrying the last block.

He opened the Long Beach paper first and turned to the sports section. Tower's column was on the left of the front page of the sports section, and he looked at the picture of the columnist which was set in at the top of the column with a sense of recognition. Suddenly, he remembered why the face was familiar. Ozzie Tower was the Ozzie who had been in the bar at the restaurant the night before.

He felt a thrill of apprehension go through him at the memory, but he was sure that he had not made any damaging statements at the bar. He began to read the column, which was not nearly as well written as Oslen's.

"We were in our favorite bistro last night after the Ram-Packer game," Tower had written. "Lots of times, the Rams come in there for a snort on Sunday night to unwind from the problems and the exertions of the week and the day, and on this night, it was no exception. Several of them came in early and one came in late, and the one who came in late was none other than Spider Leggett, the new star of the Ram receiving corps."

Spider winced at the prose, but he kept reading.

"Now Spider is an old friend of ours," Tower went on. "We've known him pretty well ever since he came up to the Rams three years ago as a raw rookie, and we always thought he had it, even from the first when no one else paid much attention to him."

Spider could not remember having exchanged three words with Tower with the exception of the night before, when he did not recognize the writer and knew only vaguely that he had ever seen him before.

He tried to remember the exchange he had had with Tower in the restaurant and could recall only that it had been no more than a sentence or two. Something about how well Frog had called the game. He remembered that Tony had said that if Brad had been at quarterback, the Rams would have

111

won, and he had pointed out that Frog had called a fine game. It was then that Tower had broken in on the conversation, but he could not bring to mind just what Tower had said.

"The only problem that Spider ever had, as we saw it," the column went on, "was that Brad Thomas, for some reason or other, never liked him. We used to wonder if Spider understood why Thomas would not throw to him, but in an unguarded moment last night, he revealed all.

" 'Ozzie,' he said, 'Brad Thomas could never have called the game against Green Bay that Frog Howard did today. Frog Howard was a genius. He knew just what he was doing, and he did it better than any quarterback in the business today.' We didn't argue the matter with Spider because we think he is right. Quite a few people would agree that Thomas, no matter how big his reputation is, can't carry Howard's football as a quarterback. The best thing that ever happened to the Rams may have been that fall he took in the shower. Right, Spider?"

Spider put the paper down with a feeling of actual physical sickness. After the torture he had been through in the early part of the week with the club because of the fight with Brad, he had hoped that the incident would, in time, be forgotten and that he could resume his place as an accepted member of the team. After Brad's speech, the climate had warmed a little, but he knew that he was still regarded with suspicion by most of the players.

Since most pro football players were practical souls, he had hoped that the job he had done on Sunday would win him more acceptance. Now, with the columns by Oslen and Tower, he was afraid.

112

He opened the other Los Angeles paper, the *Herald-Examiner,* and read the opening line in Mel Durslag's column and his spirits sank even further.

"Quite a few years ago, the Rams had trouble because of what you might call the two quarterback syndrome," Durslag had written. "First they had Waterfield vs. Van Brocklin, then Van Brocklin vs. Wade, and then Wade vs. Ryan, and, although they won with Waterfield and Van Brocklin, the long run result was to prove that a club is best off with one quarterback in charge.

"Now the old bugaboo is coming back. This time it will be Thomas vs. Howard and the guy who has set this new feud off is a little man with a big heart—Spider Leggett."

Chapter 11

ALTHOUGH none of the Ram players commented on the newspaper stories the next day, Spider was aware of a renewed and deeper hostility toward him, especially on the part of the veterans. His new found friendship with Frog Howard was unaffected, and Gangel treated him with his usual carefree warmth, but players such as Tiny Ross, Mark Kram, Sandy Crichton, Flash Werner, and the rest of the old timers, made a point of ignoring him.

He thought at first that he would explain to them what had happened, then decided that it would be pointless. Besides, some of the rookies and the younger players reacted by showing a new regard for him so that he found himself with more people to talk to than at any time since he had joined the club.

The club was scheduled to play the San Francisco Forty-Niners in San Francisco the next Sunday and the coaches, although they must have been aware of the feeling the veterans entertained toward Spider, devoted all their time to the usual meticulous preparation. Once or twice, Spider was aware of Steadman's speculative regard or of a long examination by Berman, but neither man said anything to him, much to his relief. He was not sure how he would have answered any questions they might have.

The Forty-Niners were a strong club, although they did not have the extraordinary well-articulated defense of the Packers. Spider was more familiar with Jerry Tibby, the defensive back who would be covering him, than he was with most in the league, because the Rams played the Forty-Niners three times a year—one exhibition and two league games. He had played most of the time against them, even in his rookie season, because the Rams had dominated the three games.

He sat with Gangel on the short flight north to the Bay City. The club flew to San Francisco on Saturday afternoon, working out on their own practice field in Long Beach before the flight. They checked into the Jack Tar Hotel, where almost all pro clubs stayed the day before a Forty-Niner game. Dick and Spider, as usual, shared a room.

They had checked in and were unpacking when the telephone rang, and Gangel answered it.

"It's for you," he said. "I think it's Teale." Jack Teale was the talented publicity director for the Rams and although Spider did not know him well, he liked him.

"You busy?" Teale asked. "I'd like to talk to you."

"Fine," Spider replied. "You want to come down here?"

"Is Gangel there?"

"Yes, he is," Spider said.

"Why don't you come up to my room?" Teale said. "I'd like to talk to you alone, Spider. It's 1402."

"Okay," Spider said, puzzled. "I'll be right up."

"Hey," Gangel said, bowing. "You really rate now, Spider. Publicity director needs you for a big story, I bet."

"I don't know," Leggett said. "He didn't say what it was."

"Put in a good word for your old buddy," Gangel said. "Tell him we're a team."

"I'll do my best," Spider said. "He probably wants to check how to spell my name."

He knocked gently at Teale's door, and it was opened immediately. The publicity man had a suite so that he could entertain the Los Angeles writers and the writers on the the team the club was playing, and Spider walked into the living room. On a table in one corner was a selection of liquors, glasses, ice, and iced beer, and he grinned at Teale.

"You've got the best job on the club," he said, motioning to the impromptu bar. "I better take some courses in journalism."

"It's not bad," Teale admitted. "But it's got its rough spots, too, Spider. And you're about to qualify as a rough spot."

"Me?" Spider was shocked. "I've never given you a hard time, Jack. Anytime you want me for a radio, or TV show, or an interview, I'm available. Not that I'm that much in demand."

"You'll be in demand," Jack said. "That's what I want to talk to you about. Sit down."

Spider sat down and looked at Teale questioningly.

Teale mixed himself a drink and offered Spider a Coke, which he refused. The publicity man sat down and reflected a moment before he spoke.

"You know that I came up here on Tuesday ahead of the club," he said. "I have to provide the local papers with whatever material and pictures they need in their advance publicity on the game."

Spider nodded. He also knew that Teale was regarded as one of the best publicity men in sports.

"The columnists always want to know about the hot player," Teale went on. "This week, the hot players were you and Frog, so both of you got a lot of ink in San Francisco. And most of the writers want to talk to you this afternoon so they can get quotes for tomorrow's stories."

"Okay," Spider said. "I don't mind."

"Thanks," Teale said wryly. "If you did mind, you'd be the first guy I ever met didn't want publicity."

"Then what's the matter?"

Teale sipped his drink again and looked down into it.

"The big question on all the writers' minds this week has been the split on the Rams," he said. "They are all very conscious of the possibility, because the Rams have had similar splits in the past."

"What split?"

"The Thomas versus Howard split," Teale said.

Spider felt sick suddenly. Even though the veterans had shown their dislike for him during the week, he had felt that in time the controversy would blow over, and he would be back in their good graces. After the stories in the Monday papers in Los Angeles and Long Beach, the sports writers

118

had confined themselves to speculation on how well the club would do against the Forty-Niners and whether Howard could continue to carry the brunt of the Ram attack without faltering. None of them had gone back to the Howard vs. Thomas theme and none of them had singled out Spider for particular comment, other than mentioning how well he had done against the Packers.

"How can they be interested in that?" Spider asked. "Brad's not even suited up. He won't be back for another month, at least."

"That's right," Teale said. "But they have been asking me whether or not I think that he'll be able to break in again if Howard keeps on doing as well as he did last Sunday and whether or not he'll throw to you if he does break in. And several of them feel that Oslen had a point in what he said about bad blood between you and Brad."

Spider was silent, thinking.

"So what do you want me to do?" he asked finally.

"You have to talk to them," Teale said. "If it was just a matter of their talking to you about last week's game and what happened, I could have had a little press conference. I do that now and then when there is one player they are particularly interested in, but I don't think it would be a good idea this time."

"Why not?"

"I don't think you could handle five or six of them shooting questions at you all at once about how you get along with Brad," Teale said.

"You mean you don't want me to talk to them at all?"

"No," Teale said. "You have to talk to them. But we'll take them one at a time, and I'll be with you. They'll come up here, and I'll call you when I want you. As far as you are concerned, you and Brad are old buddies, and you didn't notice any difference in the game with Frog in last week. Okay?"

"Sure," Spider told him, relieved. "Anything I can do."

He turned to go, and a thought struck him.

"They're bound to ask me how come Frog threw so many balls to me when Brad ignored me," he said. "What do I tell them?"

"Tell them it was the Green Bay defense," Teale said. "It won't make any difference in the Forty-Niner defense. They're set by now, and they're probably going to double-team you all day tomorrow anyway."

"I'll remember," Spider said.

It was a long afternoon for him. Four times he made the trip up to Teale's suite to talk to San Francisco writers and repeated the same answers to the same questions. Some of the writers, like Bob Brachman of the *Examiner*, were insistent and seemed not to believe him when he repeated over and over that there was no bad blood between him and Thomas. Brachman probed him about the bruise on his jaw and told Spider that he had gone over the movies himself and seen no evidence of the injury occurring in the game before the Packer game, but Spider insisted stubbornly that it had been a game-incurred hurt.

He pulled up his T-shirt and showed Brachman the spreading green and purple bruise over his ribs which was a relic of Aldridge's elbow block in the Packer game.

"I don't know if you saw me get this one last week," he said. "Aldridge gave me a shot just as I made a cut and nearly knocked me down, but it didn't take me out of the game. You get shots like this in every game you play."

"Not in the head," Brachman said.

"I'm sorry," Spider told him. "That's all I can tell you."

When it was all over and he had finished the last interview, he looked at Teale inquisitively.

"Was it all right?" he asked.

"I think so," Teale said. "Most of them have already written their columns so all they'll do on the interviews, if anything, is a short feature. Or they may insert a few paragraphs in the game story. I don't see how they can get anything damaging out of what you said."

"I hope you're right," Spider said. "Can I go now?"

"Sure," Teale said. "Thanks, Spider." He looked at Leggett for a few moments as if debating with himself, then held out his hand. Spider took it, surprised.

"Good luck," Teale said. "I think your big problem is that you don't think much before you act, Spider. Try thinking a little before you blow your stack."

"Thanks," Spider said. "I've been getting a lot of good advice lately, Jack. But I'll try to remember that."

He was irritated as he took the elevator back down to his own floor and joined Gangel, who had been watching the USC-Stanford game in Los Angeles on TV.

"How does it feel to be the man the papers want to talk to?" Dick asked.

"Lousy," Spider said.

"Trojans murdered the Indians," Gangel said. "Too bad you missed the game."

"I hope we have the same luck," Spider said. "If we blow this one, we'll be in trouble more ways than one."

"How's that?"

"I don't know," Spider said unhappily. "All the San Francisco writers seem to think that the Rams are split up into cliques. Me and you and the young ones on Frog's side and all the old ones for Brad."

"That's nuts," Dick said promptly. "Maybe the old guys are mad at you, but that doesn't mean the whole club is split up."

"I know it and you know it," Spider said. "But they don't know it."

Gangel was quiet for a few minutes, watching the roundup of college football scores on the television set. He was not basically an introspective or a thoughtful man, and his face was oddly serious as he thought.

"May be something to it," he said. "When you think about it."

Spider shook his head.

"I don't think so, Dick," he said. "I've spent a lot of time thinking about it in the last two or three days. I couldn't help it. But I still think this is just a temporary thing. The veterans are burned at me, and I don't blame them, but they got over the fight I had with Brad, and they all know how easy it is for something to come out in the paper different from the way you said it. They'll get over it. I know they will."

"Maybe they would if Brad was still playing," Gangel said. "But as long as he's out of action, it reminds them of what happened, and they blame you. And something else has happened, too, I think."

"What's that?" Spider asked apprehensively. "Someone else write a column about me?"

"No," Gangel said, his brow wrinkled in thought. "I mean,

122

I guess you noticed how the rooks and the young guys are your friends. Haven't you?"

"Sure," Spider said. "If it hadn't been for you and the rest of the rooks and some of the younger players, I'd have been pretty lonely this week. Except for Frog."

"Some of us were talking about it the other day," Gangel said. "Me and Axthelm, and Laguerre, and Creamer, and some of the others. I mean, we could see what the veterans were doing, and it kind of burned us a little. They act like they own the ball club, and the rest of us are nothing. If it could happen to you after you've played here for three years, what would happen to one of us if we did something they figured was wrong?"

Spider had not considered the effect of the veterans' ostracism of him on the other younger players. Originally, after the fight, they had joined the other players in ignoring him.

"The young players were just as mad as the old ones when I had the fight with Thomas," he said. "Even you. Nobody talked to me then, Dick. How is this different?"

Gangel was silent for two or three minutes as he thought about it.

"Well, what is different I guess is that this time it really wasn't your fault," he said slowly. "How can you help it what the writers say about you? And I think what made me mad was that they seemed to resent you getting a little ink for a change. I guess they're so used to being the big heroes that they don't like to see a new player getting all the play."

Spider thought about that briefly and remembered what Thomas had said in his defense. He considered his knowledge of the other Ram veterans and how unselfishly they had given themselves for the good of the team in the nearly three years he had played, and he shook his head.

"I don't think that's true," he said. "I think they don't care who gets the ink if it helps the club."

"How about Howard?" Gangel said. "I don't think they're happy he's doing good. They looked pretty grim after last week's game, didn't they? When you and Frog had big days."

"We lost," Spider said. "They aren't used to that."

"Let's see this week," Dick said, unbelieving. "Let's see what happens if we win, and you and Frog look good."

Chapter 12

As Spider waited on the sideline for Rocky Stebbins to kick off for the Rams, he thought that he enjoyed playing in Kezar Stadium. The San Francisco stadium was always cool, and the field was in excellent condition. Late in the game, the fog might blow in wispily from the bay, carrying with it squawking sea gulls, but he did not mind that. It was one of the better places to play in the league.

Stebbins's kickoff tumbled lazily, high and deep into the San Francisco end zone, and Spider went back to the bench as the Ram defensive club took the field. As he sat down, he thought that the stories in the papers in the morning had been fair, and none of them had added to his difficulties.

The San Francisco writers had tried to analyze the effect the new Ram attack would have on the San Francisco defense, and most of them had foreseen disaster. Spider had been flattered by their assessment of the improvement he made in the Ram attack; most of them had taken the position that with his sudden flowering, the loss of Thomas was offset, and the Rams would be as tough as ever. He hoped that they were right.

The big and mobile Ram defensive line stopped the Forty-Niners cold in their first series, and after three downs, which gained two yards, the San Francisco club punted. Spider came to the sideline with the rest of the team to watch the runback. Rabbit Laguerre took it on the Ram 30-yard line, dropped the ball, picked it up, hesitated a moment, then ducked under a diving high tackle by a San Francisco player.

For a moment, Spider thought that he was going to be nailed in his tracks, but Rabbit gave ground, dropping back ten yards as he tried to reach the sideline. Suddenly a lane opened down the side, and he was off, faking by another tackler as he began the run, then using blockers adroitly as he raced down a narrow path along the sideline in front of the Ram bench. He cut to his left at midfield, and, for a moment, he seemed to be gone, until a desperate Forty-Niner tipped his foot with a reaching tackle, and he fell at the San Francisco 43-yard line.

"Way to go, Rabbit," Spider said as he passed the rookie back coming off the field. Rabbit had been one of the players who had made a point of talking to him while the veterans were cutting him dead.

Rabbit nodded and grinned.

"Go get 'em," he said.

In the huddle, Frog had none of the hesitance which had

marked his first appearance the week before. He was assured and certain as he made the call, a drive off tackle by Flash Werner. Spider's assignment was to occupy the attention of the corner back by faking a pass pattern, and he ran his fake hard. The play gained six yards, and Howard was ready with the next call as soon as the offense had formed the huddle.

He called the play, and the team broke, and as Spider went out to his post near the sideline, he had to force himself to relax and not give away the call. It was the deep post which had scored on Green Bay, and he did not want to appear too anxious. You got to be an actor, he told himself, and tried not to look up to see where the corner back was playing him.

On the first running play, Spider had simply slanted to the outside to carry the back away from where Flash would hit the line. The play had taken place so quickly that he had learned nothing from the defender's reaction, and he knew now that he might be running into double coverage, if Teale had been right.

He broke fast on the snap signal and watched the corner back, who was playing him up tight. He faked to the outside and the corner back went with him, and he recognized zone coverage, which would mean that the safety would be taking him deep in the corner, and the other safety would probably pick him up on the post pattern.

He cut back to the inside again and sprinted hard, and the safety in the other deep zone came over to pick him up. He gave the defender a head fake back to the outside and kept on the post pattern, then looked back over his shoulder. The ball was dropping toward him, and this time he did not have to reach. It fell easily into his hands, and the touchdown was only a matter of running the play out.

As he went into the end zone, he threw the ball high into the air into the crowd and turned to run back to the bench. The play had been perfectly executed, and he felt the exhilaration of having done his job well. Stebbins and Ted Stefani, a rookie linebacker who blocked for extra points, slapped him on the back as he went by. Grut and Nathan, the offensive guards, trotted by him without saying anything. Both of them were old-timers.

On the sideline, Frog put out his hand and grinned widely.

"Nice catch," he said. "And a great pattern. I couldn't see you when I let the ball go, but you were right where you were supposed to be."

"So was the pass," Spider told him. "No way to miss that one, Frog."

He sat down on the bench, and Gangel sat down by him.

"Good move," he said. "I thought for a minute the weak side safety would get in the way."

"Luck," Spider said, not believing it. "Pure luck."

The extra point was good, and again Spider went to the sideline to watch Stebbins's kickoff. Again the rookie place kicker lofted the ball deep into the San Francisco end zone, preventing a runback.

Back on the bench, Howard sat down beside Spider. He had talked to the coaches in the press box, through Brad Thomas, who manned the sideline telephone during his injury.

"Dickey figures we can move on slants and sidelines," he said. "The bomb probably made them gun-shy on the long ball."

"I can beat him either way," Spider said. "If they go to man-to-man, he's deep-ball scared. He hasn't got the speed

128

to go deep with me, so they'll either zone, or he'll play me way back."

"We'll test them next time," Frog said.

Again the Ram defense held, and this time Laguerre called for a free catch and caught the ball on the Ram 35-yard line. As he passed Spider on the way to the sideline, he said, "Sorry for that. I figured you could make up the difference."

Spider grinned at him and held up a circled thumb and forefinger.

"Don't worry," he said.

Howard knelt quickly and snapped out the play, a sweep with Tilson carrying the ball to Spider's side. He lined up, cut in fast and hard at the snap and blind-sided the corner linebacker just as he was about to cut to the outside to turn the play in. Tilson lowered his shoulder and bowled over the safety man coming up, then ran for another twenty yards before he was hauled down.

He looked at Spider and smiled slightly as he came back to the huddle. In spite of the friendship he had shown after the fight with Thomas, he had joined the rest of the veterans in ignoring Spider during the past week.

"Same play," Frog said. "On two."

This time Spider hit the linebacker too high and bounced off, and the linebacker slanted out and to his left and picked up Skeeter four yards deep on the sweep. Spider knew that he could never take out the 250-pound linebacker with his meager 172 pounds if the linebacker anticipated the play, as he had this time. Tilson did not look at him this time as they returned to the huddle. It was second and 6 on the Forty-Niner 41-yard line.

Frog called a slant in to Spider, and Spider trotted out to

his position near the sideline as nonchalantly as he could manage. The defensive back was playing him tight as they lined up.

If he were to take Spider immediately on the slant in, it was unlikely that the play would work, since he had only two or three steps to take to cover Spider. The pattern called for Spider to slant toward the middle of the line as soon as the ball was snapped, but he knew that the defender would be very wary of him to the outside, and he decided that he would give the defensive back a quick outside fake before he ran the pattern. He and Frog had worked on this move in their sessions after practice, and he hoped that Howard would remember it.

The snap call came while he was thinking, and he made the outside fake immediately, then broke inside on the slant pattern, a fraction of a count late. The back bought the fake to the outside and was two steps behind Spider when Frog rifled the ball to him. The weak side linebacker loomed in front of Spider, and he cut sharply to the outside and turned on speed.

Now the safety was jockeying for position in front of him, hoping to pin him to the sideline long enough for help to arrive. Spider knew that the safety would expect him to fake to the inside and break out, and he threw a quick inside fake and faked to the outside with his hips almost at the same time. The safety overreacted to the outside, and Spider slanted toward the center of the field.

The strong side safety had gone with Shrake, the tight end, toward the other sideline, and he was out of the play. The other corner back was coming across the field on a long slant, hoping to cut Spider off before he could reach the end zone, and Spider cut back toward his left, to the sideline. The corner back had the angle on him, and he knew that he would be pinned at the ten.

He thought he might cut back there and avoid the tackle, but Gangel came from somewhere and cut the corner back down, and he scored easily. Again he threw the ball into the crowd, and he laughed aloud as he turned to trot back to the bench.

Gangel caught up with him and shook his hand.

"You keep catching, and I keep blocking, and you'll be All-Pro," he said, laughing.

The extra point team was streaming on the field, and Stebbins slapped Spider's palm as he went by.

"Keep going," he said. "I may lead the league in scoring."

"I hope so," Spider said. If the extra point and field goal kicker led the league in scoring, the Rams would have scored enough touchdowns and field goals to win the championship.

Again Frog sat down beside him after he had consulted with the coaches in the press box through Thomas.

"I'm glad you read me," Spider said. "I had to make the outside move early to make him drop off a little. If I had slanted right away, he would have been on top of me."

"I saw it," Frog said. "Comes from working after practice. I can tell when you mean a fake or when you're making a move. It helps."

"It sure does," Spider said.

Stebbins popped up on the kickoff this time, and the ball came down on the San Francisco twenty. A fullback in the wedge ahead of the kickoff returners fielded it and returned it ten yards to the Forty-Niner thirty, before he was buried in a small mountain of Ram tacklers.

131

This time the Forty-Niners, using short passes and their big, strong running backs, moved the ball to the Ram 32-yard line before they were stopped. The field goal made the score 14-3 for the Rams with the first quarter nearly over.

"All the way, baby," Laguerre said to Spider as he prepared to take the field to handle the kickoff. "I hope they kick it to me."

Unfortunately for the Forty-Niners, they did. This time Rabbit took the ball four yards in the end zone and burst straight up the middle. The wedge opened a crack in the Forty-Niner defense, and he was through it in a flash. The kicker forced him to cut to the sideline and hesitate a moment, and then he cut back and slanted across the field. He was caught on the Forty-Niner 16-yard line by the pursuit, making up ground on his evasive tactics.

"Just a short one this time," he said to Spider as he left the field. "No problem."

Howard sent Werner and Tilson into the line twice, but the Forty-Niner defense had tightened, and they managed only four yards between them. It was third and 6 on the San Francisco twelve when he called the play for the third down.

It was a play action pass, and Spider was surprised when he heard it. The Forty-Niners would be expecting a pass on third and 6, and the fake of the run would probably be ignored. The pass would go to him on a quick slant over the middle after the fake of the fullback up the center. The fake should bring the middle linebacker in, but the Forty-Niner middle linebacker had been in the league a long time.

Spider lined up closer to the tackle than usual, so that his route over the middle would be a short one. At the snap, he took off at top speed, aiming at the corner of the field on the opposite side. The corner back went with him, a step deeper. As he reached the target area, he saw that the middle linebacker had dropped back in perfect position to cut off a pass over the middle. The secondary, this close to the Forty-Niner goal line, was crowded.

Spider cut sharply back to his left and looked for the ball. Frog had evaded a Forty-Niner rush and was swinging wide in the same direction Spider was running. He saw Spider and motioned for him to go deeper, and Spider turned downfield and raced into the end zone. Again he looked back, and this time the ball was coming on a hard, flat line, and it thudded into his arms and chest as a tackler hit him and drove him to the ground.

He climbed to his feet and heard the crowd booing and knew that he had scored again, and this time he was too shaken up to throw the ball into the crowd. He dropped it to the ground, started back toward the sideline, and was lifted and shaken. When he was put down again, he saw that Bob Creamer, the rookie tackle who had replaced Hoy Yuen, was clapping him on the back.

"Little man!" Creamer yelled. "Way to go, little man!"

By the half, the score was 28-3. Spider had not caught another touchdown pass; this time Howard had hit Gangel while the Forty-Niners were overly concerned with covering Spider. In the second half, the game rapidly became a rout. Spider caught eight passes in the third period, then left the game as Steadman tried Rabbit Laguerre at spread end. Squirming Herman Weiskopf replaced Gangel at flanker, and the Ram attack slowed down. With the score 49-10, Steadman put Axthelm in at quarterback, and the game was over. The

Forty-Niners scored on a desperate long pass with seconds left, and the final score was 49-17.

In the dressing room, Spider felt fresh and strong. He had sat out most of the fourth period, and he had scored three touchdowns, and nothing could have made him feel better.

The writers flocked around him, and he tried to listen to their questions and answer them honestly, but he was not sure that he had, when it was all over.

"You caught 13 for three touchdowns and 280 yards," Florence said to him at one point. "How do you feel about that?"

Spider looked at the pudgy *Los Angeles Times* writer and smiled.

"Good," he said. "How else?"

"This is the second big week you have had with Howard," Florence said. "How about that?"

"Hooray for Frog," Spider said, happily.

Chapter 13

On the flight back to Los Angeles, Spider sat with Howard and went over some of the patterns which had not worked too well against San Francisco. Howard diagrammed the moves on the back of the menu, and Spider showed him how the defense had reacted to them, and the two of them devised methods for correcting the faults. After the Tuesday morning meeting, Howard would make the suggestions to Berman, the offensive coach. Berman might pick the ideas apart, but he was always a thoughtful and receptive listener.

Spider had been happy to discover that Howard had no reluctance about throwing into double coverage. Often a second quarterback, unaccustomed to seeing such close covering, was not sure enough of himself to risk a pass which had to be perfectly thrown if it were not to be intercepted.

"I was afraid a few times that you wouldn't throw to me," he said. "They were taking me in and out and short and long, and I was only open for a split second. Lots of quarterbacks would go to another receiver or eat the ball rather than throw into coverage like that."

Howard looked at him and laughed.

"I learned a long time ago to take what I can get," he said. "If you have confidence in yourself, it's no harder to throw the ball into tight coverage than it is to throw it anywhere else. As long as I can anticipate your moves, I can lead you away from the defensive back, anyway. And I know that if I get the ball in reach, you'll catch it."

"Thanks," Spider said. "That's not exactly a unanimous opinion." He was thinking of the reasons Brad Thomas had given him for not throwing to him more often.

It was dark when the plane landed in Los Angeles, and Spider was tired. Although he had taken almost as much of a physical beating against the Forty-Niners as he had against the Packers, he felt none of the soreness that had followed the Green Bay game. He picked up his overnight case, headed for his car, and thought that the trainer had no liniment in his bag as effective as winning, in easing the aches and pains of a tough game.

He drove slowly on the freeway to Long Beach, listening to the car radio and enjoying the aftermath of the good afternoon. In his mind, he went over the balls he had caught, and the moves he had made, and he knew that he need have no worry about his pro football future now. Even if the Rams did trade him when this season was over, he thought, there should be plenty of other clubs anxious to get him.

The newspapers the next morning harped again on the new found Ram offensive power, based on the team of Howard to Leggett, and Spider read with relish the words of praise about his game. Both the Los Angeles papers carried stories questioning whether or not Thomas would be able to dislodge Howard when his hand healed.

"Thomas will be back for the last game of the season," Oslen wrote. "That is the game which could decide the Coastal Division championship because the Rams play their principal rivals, the Baltimore Colts, in Baltimore. What will Steadman do if Frog Howard continues to look as good as he has in the last two games? Will he still go to Thomas simply because Thomas has been the number one quarterback for the Rams for the last seven years? And if he decides to start Brad, what will he do? It seems inconceivable that he would still be reluctant to throw to Spider Leggett, who has shown convincingly that all he needed was someone to believe in him. Leggett is the best receiver on the club now and one of the two or three best in the league. Coach Steadman has a problem, and it will be interesting to see how he works it out."

The problem did not arise during the next three weeks, since Brad's hand kept him on the bench. The Rams won all three games easily, and Spider's streak of good games continued. He caught 12 passes against the Chicago Bears for two touchdowns, then came back against the Atlanta Falcons to catch 15 for three touchdowns and over 300 yards. Then the Rams met the Cleveland Browns, one of the powers of the East, and a team with what was considered to be the second-best pass defense in the two Eastern Divisions.

The game was played in Cleveland's Municipal Stadium on a bitter cold, windy day, the kind of day calculated to stifle the passing game.

"If the weather in Cleveland is as bad as the forecast would indicate," Florence wrote in his pre-game story, "the Rams may not be able to depend on the air game as much as they have in recent weeks. It is doubtful if even the team of Frog Howard to Spider Leggett can operate effectively in 15-degree weather on a frozen field with a 30-mile-an-hour wind blowing. If they can, against the kind of pass defense the Browns mount, they are the supermen some writers are calling them already."

Frog and Spider talked the problem of cold over in the locker room before the game. As usual, Spider was wearing a short-sleeved jersey so that he could feel the impact of the ball on his bare arms rather than through the material of sleeves.

"Maybe you better put on a long-sleeved shirt," Frog said. "Your arms will probably be so numb that you won't be able to feel the ball anyway."

"No," Spider said stubbornly. "It wasn't too bad during the warmup. I don't want to change a winning combination now, Frog."

"Look," Frog told him. "If I'm going to get the ball to you through this wind, I'm going to have to wing it, Spider. It'll be coming as hard as I can throw it so the wind won't carry it too much. You'll need all the padding you can get."

"Just throw it," Spider told him. "I'll catch it."

Frog led the club to a 35-14 victory over the Browns, and

138

he hit Spider with 10 passes, two of them long, with the wind, for touchdowns. By the time the game was over, Spider's bare arms were as blue as the Rams' road jerseys, but he had felt no pain during the excitement of the contest. It was not until he stepped under the warm shower in the dressing room that he felt the sting in his arms and hands, and by then it did not matter.

The prickling in the skin of his arms lasted only a few moments and by the time he had toweled himself vigorously and returned to his locker, he had forgotten it.

Florence and a couple of the Cleveland writers were waiting for him.

"Did the cold bother you much?" Mal asked and Spider shook his head.

"I didn't notice it at all when we were in action," he said truthfully. "The only time I was really aware of it was when we had to stop for the TV time-outs and stand around for two minutes."

"How about your hands?" asked Chuck Heaton. Heaton was a knowledgeable, friendly writer for a Cleveland paper.

Spider held them out for inspection. They were red and a little puffy from the cold.

"They bother me more right now than they did during the game," he said. "I thought I might have been frost bitten, but Doc says not."

"Wasn't it hard to hold the ball?" Heaton insisted.

"No harder than usual," Spider said. "I tucked my hands into the front of my pants between plays so that they weren't exposed that much."

"It looked like Frog was drilling the ball," Florence said. "Was that because of the wind?"

"He had to," Spider told him. "I don't know any other quarterback in football who could have done a better job of throwing into the wind than Frog did today. He's got a real strong arm, and he needed it."

"How about Thomas?" Mal asked.

"I don't know," Spider said frankly. "I've never played with him under conditions like the ones we played under today. But he doesn't throw as heavy a ball as Frog does, normally."

"Maybe that is just because he's afraid to throw hard yet," Florence said. Thomas had been working out for a week, testing his hand, and he had not thrown the ball with his usual crisp accuracy. Since he had not been working with the club in offensive drills, Spider did not know how hard he was throwing.

"I'm not talking about now," Spider said. "He's just warming up easy so as not to hurt the hand again. I mean before he was hurt, he threw a softer ball than Frog. That doesn't mean he can't wing the ball when he wants to."

"I see," Florence said slowly.

On the flight back to Los Angeles, Brad sat down beside Spider for a few moments. Their relationship over the weeks since Brad's injury had been one of guarded acceptance, without the warmth of friendship. Spider was still grateful to the veteran quarterback for having gone to bat for him with the team, but he could not make himself forget that Thomas had told him that he had no confidence in Spider's ability as a receiver.

"Anyone sitting here?" Thomas asked before he sat down.

"Frog," Spider said. "But he's back in the lounge playing hearts, I think. Sit down."

Thomas sat down in the aisle seat and leaned back. He

140

looked at his right hand and clenched it. On the back a small lump marked the broken knuckle, but the hand seemed strong enough. Thomas had big, powerful hands, and Spider involuntarily looked at his own. People were always surprised at how small they were.

"How's the hand?" he asked Brad.

"Getting stronger," Brad said. "Doc says I'll be able to play next Sunday against the Colts, if it works out all right in practice this week."

"Good," Spider said. His voice sounded insincere even to himself, and he could not help feeling a small thrill of apprehension. If Thomas returned to action, the short, lively stardom of Spider Leggett might come to a halt.

"That's what I wanted to talk to you about," Thomas said bluntly. "I know you don't like me, Spider, but I don't want you to think that that will have anything to do with our relationship on the field."

"What do you mean?" Spider said. "I like you all right."

"Thanks," Brad said, smiling thinly. "But don't bother to pretend, Spider. You may get over it in time, but right now I'd bet my share of the Super Bowl money you're hoping the hand doesn't come around in time for me to start."

Spider was silent for a few minutes, considering what Thomas had said. The veteran, of course, was right. Spider's relationship with Frog Howard was a good one, and he had faith in Howard's ability to move the club plus appreciation for Howard's confidence in him. He decided that there was no point in hiding the fact from Thomas.

"You're right," he said at last. "I'm glad your hand is better, but I hope that Frog stays in, Brad. We've been doing all right with him in there. Better than we did when you were."

141

"He's a fine quarterback," Brad said sincerely. "And he's a good friend of mine, Spider. But if I can beat him out as number one, you can bet your boots I will. And if I can, the Rams will be a better ball club for it."

"I don't think you can," Spider said in a flash of anger and loyalty to Howard. "Maybe once you were better, Brad, but not now. He's come a long way."

"Well, that's not what I wanted to talk about, anyway," Brad said. "I'd be the last guy to low rate Frog. I wanted to ask you if you will work with me after practice, the way you do with Howard."

"Why?" Spider asked in surprise.

"I talked to Frog about it," Brad said. "It's all right with him. He doesn't need the work anymore, and I do, and I think I should get used to your moves as well as he has. If I'm going to take over at quarterback again, then I don't want the team to lose any efficiency because I can't use you as well as Frog has."

"I don't know," Spider said slowly. "I don't think it would be fair to Frog, Brad. I mean he was the guy who volunteered to come out and work with me when no one else would give me the time of day. Why should I quit on him and start working with you?"

"Because you play on a team," Brad said. "I think in the last few weeks you have begun to forget that, Spider. I'm not asking to work with you for my personal benefit. Without being too blunt about it, I don't have to work with you to stay with this club. But if I have to play with you, it could be the difference between our winning and losing a championship. Think it over."

He got up and walked down the aisle quickly, leaving

Spider staring after him. During the weeks that he and Frog had been playing well, the veterans on the club had maintained their cool disregard for Spider, and now he thought he understood why. He had hoped that they would forgive and forget, but instead they had withdrawn even more, leaving Spider and the younger players more and more to their own devices. Before the break, the older players had made it a point to help the younger ones master the subtleties of their positions, but in recent weeks the club had more and more divided into what, for want of another name, could be called the Howard and the Thomas camps. The veterans gave the impression that they were only too anxious to get Brad back. They were superb professionals, and so far their performances on the field had not suffered, but the cohesion and team spirit which had marked the team under Thomas seemed to be coming apart.

If Thomas had been influencing them against him and, by implication, against Frog, he could understand their attitudes better. They had spent most of their lives as professional football players taking orders from Brad on the field and looking up to him as their leader off the field.

He discussed Brad's request with Frog when the big quarterback came back to fold himself uncomfortably into his seat, and he was surprised to find that Frog was all in favor of it.

"I think it's a good idea," he said. "Brad will need the extra work to get his arm in shape, and you and I can work together during the regular team practice anyway. It'll be good for you to get used to Brad's ball again, and he knows a lot more about patterns and moves than I do, Spider."

Spider was surprised at the big man's complacency. He had

143

supposed that Frog would feel the same way about Brad's return as he did, and he said so.

Frog looked at him with amazement.

"You figure I'm jealous of Brad?" he asked, shocked. "Look, I'll do everything I can to keep the number one job, Spider, but when I came up to this club, no one helped me more than Brad Thomas. You may not like him because you think he slighted you when he was quarterback, but I might have done the same thing if you had dropped as many balls for me as you did for him, Spider. If he comes back at full strength, I expect I'll be back on the bench. I won't like it and in time, if it goes on, I might ask to be traded to a club where I can be number one, but I won't resent Brad because of that."

"You mean that you admit he's a better quarterback than you are?"

Frog laughed.

"No," he said, "I don't think anyone is a better quarterback than I am. But he's had more experience, and he may run this ball club better than I can."

"How can you say that?" Spider asked. "Look what we've done since you took over. He wasn't moving the team half as well as you do."

"Maybe," Frog said. "Maybe a lot of things were ready to fall in place when he got hurt. Maybe he would have gone back to throwing to you because you were getting single coverage. He probably would. One thing sure would not have happened if he hadn't been hurt."

"What's that?" Spider asked.

"The club would not have started to break up into cliques," Frog said. "I haven't said anything about it because I don't

144

want to make it an issue. But do me a favor, will you, Spider?"

"Sure," Spider said. "Whatever you want."

"Work with him as hard as you did with me," Frog said, his long face serious. "And don't take the veterans' attitude so seriously. Let's try to make this ball club one club again instead of two."

Chapter 14

Aᴄᴛᴜᴀʟʟʏ, Spider worked with both Frog and Brad. Gangel joined them, ostensibly to take some of the load off Spider but really in order to sharpen his own skills. They worked for fifteen or twenty minutes after practice, and Spider was surprised at the easy camaraderie between Thomas and Howard. The two quarterbacks worked together and discussed their problems with the familiarity of old friends. They included Spider and Dick just as easily, and Spider found himself looking forward to their extracurricular sessions.

The rest of the veterans still regarded him with suspicion and distaste, however. And the rookies and younger players rallied to his cause because they had known the same feeling of loneliness which had troubled him. It was natural for the younger players to associate with one another, but usually this did not lead to a feeling of antagonism between the groups.

With the division championship riding on the final game of the season against the Colts, whatever intrasquad problems simmered underneath the ordered routine of practice were subordinated to the business of preparation.

Brad was throwing strongly now, and Spider recognized the fact that the veteran quarterback was a more polished passer than Howard. He had the faculty for matching the pass to the pattern to a finer degree than Howard; he could float a ball to a receiver or fire it like a bullet, and in either case, it was always precisely on target. He could anticipate his target, too, although at first, he was not able to read Spider's moves as well as Frog.

"You're quicker than I remembered," he told Spider on Friday afternoon as they walked back across the practice field to the dressing room. Although he and Spider discussed technical matters freely, Spider still felt that Brad had reservations about him. Spider admired the quarterback's dedication and his football knowledge and skill, but he could not help resenting the fact that his return could very well mean that Frog would be on the bench against Baltimore.

"You run your paterns sharper, and you don't lose any speed after you have made your cut," he went on. "You used to have a tendency to make the cut and slow down to look for the ball. When you did, the defensive back had time to recover and get in position to knock the ball down."

"Dickey told me the same thing," Spider said shortly. "I've been working on it. Frog has spent a lot of time with me."

"I would have worked with you if you had asked me," Brad said quietly. "I used to work with Terry and Lyman, Spider. One of the reasons we worked together so well was that they did the same thing with me you are doing with Frog."

"Why didn't you say so then?"

"You didn't ask me," Brad said. "After a while, I got the feeling that you hated my guts, Spider."

"I did," Spider said.

"I told you why I had to go to other receivers," Brad said. "I'd do the same thing again, Spider."

Spider looked at him wordlessly and walked ahead of Thomas into the dressing room. He did not trust himself to reply to Brad; his frustration and anger at Brad's distrust of him as a receiver, early in the season, were still too fresh in his mind for him to discuss the matter philosophically.

As he showered and dressed, he wondered which quarterback Steadman would start against Baltimore. The head coach had made no announcement, although the Los Angeles writers had been after him to commit himself.

"It depends on how Brad's hand responds to work," Steadman said. "If I think he's ready, he starts. He is still the number one quarterback on the Rams."

Spider had thought that Steadman's blunt statement was unwise and that it could do nothing but harm to Howard's attitude during the week, but Frog accepted it easily. Spider had thought that Howard was hiding his true feeling when he had said on the plane that he was resigned to taking a back seat to Thomas if Brad came back, but if that were true, Frog hid his feelings very well.

Saturday morning, before the team took the field for the

short warmup which ended their preparations, Steadman called for their attention in the locker room.

"So you will all know before you read it in the papers," he said. "Brad will start at quarterback. That's all."

His words started a quick hum of low-pitched conversation. Several of the older players made a point of going over to Brad's locker and shaking his hand or slapping his back. Frog grinned at him and shook his hand, too. Spider, although he had forced himself to recognize the possibility that Brad's return would break up his teaming with Howard, tried to hide the quick rush of disappointment and dismay the announcement created in him. The other young players accepted the announcement quietly, but few of them said anything to Thomas.

"On the field," Steadman said, breaking up the conversations. "Let's go."

They left the locker room in a clatter of cleats on the wooden floor, and Spider found himself walking with a group of rookies and second- and third-year players. He had not realized before that the team had so clearly separated into two components. The veterans were in a group of their own, walking ahead.

"How about that?" Bob Creamer, the big rookie tackle, said disgustedly. "Why change a winning combination?"

"He's the old head," Rabbit Laguerre said. The fleet running back shrugged. "You know coaches. They go with the guys they know the best. No matter how good anyone else looks."

Slow Boyle, a second-year center, shook his head.

"Makes you wonder what you have to do to break in," he

said. "Frog's been going like a house afire, and what good did it do him?"

"None," Spider said. "Not a bit. And the funny thing is they don't really know if Brad is ready or not. He's throwing good, but he hasn't been in a game for six weeks."

"Nothing we can do about it," Gangel said, cheerfully. "If Brad can't cut it, I expect they'll go back to Frog in a hurry, anyway."

"That might be too late," Spider said.

The news was in the early edition of the Sunday papers, and the reaction of the Los Angeles writers was mixed. Bob Oates, the *Herald Examiner*'s astute writer who had been covering the Rams for more years than Spider had been alive, agreed with Steadman.

"Howard has done better than anyone could have expected," Oates wrote. "But Brad Thomas has a history of winning big games, and if his hand is all right, you can expect him to win another one. Howard is wonderful insurance for the future, but Thomas is the tested man."

Oslen, on the other hand, deplored Steadman's lack of perception.

"Since Howard took over the Ram offense," he wrote, "the club has come to life. The Rams were averaging a meager 17 points per game before Thomas was injured, and their aerial attack had, for all practical purposes, been grounded. Since Howard has taken over, the change has been a dramatic one. The club's average is over 30 points per game, and once again the Ram passing attack is the most feared in the league. Why disturb a successful formula?"

Most of the comment agreed with Oslen and the radio and TV sports commentators were almost unanimous in their

151

criticisms of Steadman. One of them even went so far as to suggest that Steadman had grown too set and habit ridden in his long stint as head coach and that Dan Reeves, the club owner, should consider a change.

Mal Florence, the *Times* writer who handled the pre-game story, was noncommital. "Steadman undoubtedly knows more about his team than we do," he wrote. "Some of you may not believe this, but it is true. Only the game itself can tell whether he is right or wrong."

The big cement bowl was jammed by kickoff. The game itself would have been enough to fill it; the controversy in the press about the relative merits of the Ram quarterbacks created even more excitement.

During the three years Spider had spent with the Rams, the crowds had been friendly at home. The Rams had been consistent winners and even in their few losses at home, the Ram fans had shown a strong loyalty for their club. Spider had heard a few boos directed toward him after his early bad games, but the booers had long since turned into enthusiastic supporters.

Certainly one of the favorites of the Ram crowds, in victory or defeat, had always been Brad Thomas. The quarterback had brought Los Angeles three championships in the seven years he had run the team, and he was generally recognized, since the retirement of Bart Starr of Green Bay and John Unitas of the Baltimore Colts, the best quarterback in pro football. Even though he still resented Brad's usurping Frog's starting position at quarterback, Spider could understand why Steadman would choose him to start so crucial a game. Howard had been great for six weeks, but Thomas had been the best for that many years.

So Spider was shocked at the reception Brad Thomas got when he was introduced at the beginning of the game. He was used to hearing a swelling roar of applause when the Ram quarterback was announced and began his leisurely trot to the middle of the field. Although Flash Werner and Skeeter Tilson and some of the other veterans were always greeted enthusiastically, it was Brad who brought the crowd to their feet.

This time, when the public address system boomed "And at quarterback, Brad Thomas!" the volume of sound was the same, but it was almost evenly mixed between cheers and boos.

Spider was already on the field, standing with the rest of the Ram offensive team, when the introduction was made. He searched Thomas's face as the quarterback came to the team and shook hands with Werner and Tilson, but Brad showed no emotion.

"Let's go," he said. The team ran a dummy play and raced to the sideline, where the whole club huddled for a moment before the kickoff.

"All right," Steadman said, in the middle of the circle of players. "It all comes down to today. Don't kick it away."

Laguerre took a low, skidding kickoff on the Ram 12-yard line and burst straight up the middle of the field. The wedge of Ram blockers cleared out the middle of the Colt defense, and suddenly Laguerre sliced into the clear at the Ram 30-yard line and slanted to his right, toward the Ram bench. Spider was standing on the sideline and the flying back spirited by, within two yards of him.

"Go, baby, go," someone yelled behind Spider, and he found that he, too, was howling at Rabbit. Rabbit faked in

153

as the safety man in the kickoff defense slanted over to pin him to the sideline, then cut back to the sideline and lifted over the safety's desperate tackle and was in the clear.

The roar of the crowd was almost deafening as Laguerre trotted back to the sideline to be engulfed by his teammates.

"No sweat," he hollered, capering happily. "No sweat!"

As it turned out, he was completely wrong. The Colts, behind their young quarterback, came back quickly to tie the score, and the Ram attack, which had operated with smooth precision under Frog Howard, operated with something less than that under Brad Thomas. He called the plays with the same sure authority that he had always demonstrated, but the timing in their executions was a vital split second off and the split second was enough.

The first time the Ram offense started a series, it was from the 20-yard line and Thomas, with his usual daring, called a long pass to Spider. Spider knew that he expected the Colt defense to blitz, sending in one or two linebackers to test the quarterback after his long absence from contact.

The Colts obliged, and Spider ran a quick hitch and go on the defensive back, who was isolated on him with the linebacker on his side gone, and the safety concerned with Flash Werner, who had circled out of the backfield as another receiver. Spider ran straight at the defender, stopped as if to hook for a short pass, then turned and accelerated as the back came up. He was three steps in the clear when he looked back for the ball.

It was high and soft, and he had to slow down to wait for it and just as he reached, the defensive back leaped high and batted it away with a desperate hand. Spider trotted back to the huddle, and he could not help thinking that if Frog had been the quarterback, the play would have been good for a touchdown or a long gain.

He glanced at Brad as he knelt in the huddle, but the quarterback showed no emotion. He called the next play matter-of-factly, a turn-out pass to Gangel, and said nothing to Spider about how the ball had been thrown.

Gangel caught the ball, but it was for only a 4-yard gain, since it had been thrown a trifle behind him, causing him to break stride and allowing a linebacker to reach him.

With third and 6, Thomas called a quick look in to Slats Shrake, the giant tight end. He hit Shrake a split second too soon and Shrake, although he held the ball, was hauled down shy of the first down, and the Rams had to punt. As the offensive team left the field, there was a scattering of boos.

The boos grew as the game went on. The Ram defense kept them in the game through the first half as the offense sputtered and failed to move the ball, and in the second period, the fans began to chant.

"We want Frog!" they yelled. "We want Frog!"

Thomas, although he must have heard the chant as clearly as anyone else, seemed totally unaffected by it. He went about the business of calling the game as precisely and intelligently as always, but the minute faults in execution continued to turn potential gaining plays to failures. At the half, the score was 17-7 for Baltimore, and Spider was seething with anger.

"What does he need?" he asked Gangel as they left the field for the half-time intermission. "When is he going to put Frog in?"

155

He did not have to wait long for the answer. After going over the errors of omission and commission the Rams had perpetrated during the first half and diagramming a few changes for the second half, Steadman paused for a moment.

"Same teams," he said. "Except Howard starts at quarterback."

Spider glanced quickly at Thomas to see how the veteran quarterback would accept this, but Thomas's face showed nothing. He slapped Frog on the back and said "Good luck, Frog," but his face was impassive.

Whether it was the adjustments that the Ram coaching staff had made at the half or the improved timing of the attack under Howard, the game turned entirely in the second half. The Ram defense held up as well as ever, but the Ram offense was moving the ball now. The first offensive series, Frog called the same play that Brad had called to open, and this time the long pass on the hitch and go dropped exactly into Spider's hands, and he was away for the touchdown on a 68-yard sprint that lifted the crowd in roaring acclaim.

Spider had caught only two passes in the first half; in the second, he caught nine more, and the Ram passing attack, which had suffered as much as the rest of the offense, suddenly became as lethal as it had been in their drive down the stretch. By the middle of the fourth period, Los Angeles led by three touchdowns, and Steadman felt confident enough to put Axthelm in at quarterback.

When Spider came off the field with three minutes to play and the game won, the crowd came to its feet cheering him. Although he gave no sign that he heard the cheering, he savored every moment of the short trip to the sideline.

Thomas was the first man to shake his hand at the sideline.

"Great," he said, beaming. "You were something else, Spider."

Chapter 15

THE victory gave the Rams the Coastal Division championship and set them up for a divisional playoff game with the
Green Bay Packers in Milwaukee the following Sunday. The
Packers had coasted through their division, playing with the
power and drive which had marked them over the years
and, given the probability that the weather in Milwaukee
would be cold and bitter, most experts picked the Packers
to win the Western Conference title.

The reaction of the Ram fans in the game against the Colts
pointed up another reason that most sports writers made
Green Bay the favorite over the coast team. Spider was surprised, on Monday morning when he read the game stories
in the Los Angeles papers, to discover that almost as much

space was given to the development of cliques on the Ram team as to their come-from-behind victory.

"For the first time in years, the Ram fans were divided into two camps," Oslen wrote. "It brought back old times, when half the stands hollered 'We want Waterfield' and the other half hollered, just as loudly, 'We want Van Brocklin.' In this case the ones yelling for Frog Howard would seem to have had more common sense. Brad Thomas, coming off six weeks of idleness, obviously has lost some of his touch. The team did not start to jell until the second half, when Steadman reluctantly admitted his mistake and sent Frog Howard back into the game. Howard was like a transfusion for a dying man; he brought the club to life and health at once."

Ozzie Tower, the Long Beach writer who had gotten Spider into trouble to begin with, was even more outspoken.

"Maybe the Ram coaching staff won't admit it," he wrote, "but yesterday afternoon in the Coliseum, Brad Thomas demonstrated to the satisfaction of all but a few diehards that his long and illustrious career as the quarterback of the Rams is over. A new star was born in the second half against the Colts. Or maybe 'new' is the wrong word. Frog Howard has been leading the club with elan and efficiency for six weeks now, and he showed the same flair which makes him great in the second half when he took over from the aging, tired Thomas to take the Rams to the Coastal Division title. Steadman should have no doubts about who starts next week's game against the Packers in Milwaukee. It has to be Howard."

Bob Oates in the *Herald-Examiner* and Mal Florence in the *Times* were reserved in their judgments. Both of them

160

pointed out that Thomas was coming off a long period of inactivity and that his timing was off.

"It is unfair to criticize Thomas on the basis of this game," Oates said. "Time and again a play missed by the wink of an eye. Brad called a fine game. Given his usual precise timing, he would have done as well as Howard."

On the team itself, the reaction of the players was marked. If there had been a division between young and old before the Baltimore game, the game itself served to make it deeper and more serious. The youngsters gloried in Frog's accomplishments and most of them talked to Spider about it, since they had taken him as a sort of unofficial leader. Normally they would have turned to Frog Howard, the quarterback, but Howard would have none of their adulation.

"What has happened is no good," he said to Spider on Tuesday as they suited up for practice. Spider had congratulated him on his game and on the publicity he had received. He had said nothing about the split cheering for Thomas and Howard.

"I like the publicity," Howard said. "And I'm glad I had a good day. Any player who says he's not happy over a good day is a liar. But I know that Brad could have had the same day or a better one if he had been playing the last six weeks. And I don't like the feeling on the team now, Spider. We haven't had it in the four years I've been here. And from what I have heard from players on other clubs, nothing kills a team quicker than being split between old and young, offense and defense, one quarterback and another. If we're going to beat Green Bay, we better be a team."

"I'm sorry," Spider said, surprised at the vehemence of Frog's reply. "I didn't mean any harm."

161

Frog looked at him for a long time, silently.

"You never mean any harm, Spider," he said. He started to say something else and stopped.

"What does that mean?"

"Nothing," Frog answered. "Forget it."

He turned and walked away, and Spider looked after him in puzzlement.

"What's eating him?" Gangel asked and Spider shrugged.

"I don't know," he said slowly. "I thought he'd be happy this week."

"He should be," Gangel said. "I bet Steadman starts him against Green Bay."

"If he doesn't, he ought to have his head examined," Spider said. They were in the dressing room, and he had not realized that he might be overheard, and he was surprised to feel a hand on his shoulder. He turned to look up into the angry face of Tiny Ross, the massive defensive tackle who had been All-Pro for four years in a row.

"Steadman doesn't need his head examined," Ross said. "Ah can think of a few guys around here Ah'd like to hit in the head, Spider. Startin' with you."

He turned and walked away, and Spider gaped after him. Ross was a mild-mannered man who played like a demon on the field, but was as gentle as a lamb off it.

"Lots of friendly people around," Gangel said. "Looks like the old-timers don't like for anyone but their friends to get any ink, Spider."

"I haven't done anything," Spider said bitterly. "They have been on my back a long time. I hope they choke."

The practices were held in unaccustomed quiet during the week before they left for the game in Milwaukee. The veterans had almost nothing to say to the younger players, and the youngsters, defiantly, kept to themselves. Even the Los Angeles writers noticed the split on the team and began to ask questions about it.

Spider was the object of most of the questions and he said nothing. He denied that any rift had developed on the team and finally refused to discuss the matter at all.

The only rookie the veterans paid any attention to at all was Billy Gallagher, the spread end who had been on injured reserve since early in the season, when he had come down with mononucleosis. Gallagher had returned to the roster at the same time that Brad had begun working again, and he seemed none the worse for his illness. He was a big, gangling youngster with exceptional speed and sure hands. Since he had been away during the development of the feud, he took no sides.

He was a good-natured, easy going boy, and he did his best to get along with both sides. The younger players expected him to side with them, but Gallagher, showing unusual wisdom for his age, refused.

"I think you're *all* wrong," he said, his fresh young face serious. "What are you going to do? Drop the ball if Brad throws it and catch it if it's Frog's pass? Who does that hurt?"

"You're right," Spider said. "I agree with you."

"So what's the argument about?"

"I don't know," Spider said, helplessly. "I guess it got out of hand."

Gallagher, who had been standing with Spider back of the offensive team waiting for his turn to run a pattern, shook his head angrily.

"I don't understand any of it," he said. "You guys been

busting your back all year for a chance at the championship game and the Super Bowl, and all at once, you spend more time fighting each other than you do getting ready for the game. What happened?"

"It's a long story," Spider said.

"It's ridiculous," Gallagher told him. "Why don't you all just cut it out and get to work?"

"We're working," Spider said. "You're up, rook."

Gallagher took his place in the offensive huddle, and ran a pattern, and the conversation ended.

Steadman took them to Milwaukee on Thursday before the Sunday game so that they could work out in County Stadium and get a taste of the cold before game time.

"There's no point in going earlier than that," he said. "If the weather turns bad, we'll miss too much work, and there isn't enough time for anyone to get used to cold weather. I played eleven years for the Bears, and I didn't get used to it. You just have to try to ignore it."

He named Brad Thomas as the starting quarterback again, and this time Thomas performed with his old skill and aplomb. The day was bitterly cold with the thermometer hovering around fifteen degrees all through the game, but the wind was negligible, and Spider found that he did not suffer nearly as much as he had in Cleveland when the wind had blown.

County Stadium was packed; none of the Green Bay fans stayed away because of the weather. On one occasion, Spider remembered, they had filled the stadium in Green Bay with the temperature 17 degrees below zero and a 20-mile-an-hour wind blowing. The cold factor on that day—the combination of cold, wind, and humidity—had been 51 degrees below zero but it had not daunted the Green Bay fans or the team, which had beaten the Dallas Cowboys for the National Football League Championship.

The skies were clear, and the sun did its wintry best to warm the air as the Rams took the field. The Packers were kicking off, and Spider stood on the sideline with his hands tucked under his arms, trying to keep them warm. Rabbit Laguerre took the kickoff on the goal line and fought his way out to the Ram 22-yard-line before he disappeared under a pile of green jerseys.

In the huddle, Thomas snapped out the signal with authority and confidence, and the club came out with a snap and a shout. Thomas faked a hand-off to Tilson into the line, then pitched out quickly to Bob Ottum, who was swinging wide to his left. Spider slanted hard to his right and hit the Ram right corner back knee high, upending him, and clearing a route for Ottum near the sideline. The big back rumbled for sixteen yards, and Spider could feel the electricity in the huddle when he knelt for the next call. In some games, the team seemed to be in the grip of a special impetus, and he could already feel it in this game.

Brad whip-sawed the Packer defense with running plays to the inside and out, mixing in one or two short passes, and drove the team 78 yards to a touchdown, sending Skeeter Tilson booming over the middle behind a rousing block by Marty Nathan at guard for the last two yards and the touchdown. It had been a beautiful, carefully thought-out drive, and Spider, as he returned to the sideline, felt the warmth of a job well done. He had caught one short pass for a first down, but the important thing was that the team had functioned smoothly as a unit.

165

The Packers came back stubbornly, using the same type of offense, sending their big backs thumping into the giant Ram line for small gains, now and then flipping a quick sideline or look-in pass, and they tied the score with three minutes left in the quarter.

The two drives had been mounted along the ground for the most part, and Spider was surprised to look up and see that less than three minutes remained in the quarter. The ground plays, with the clock running continuously, ate up time.

Aldridge, the Packer defensive back Spider had beaten decisively in their meeting during the regular season, was playing him more cautiously in this game.

He was not playing Spider up as tight as usual and Spider knew that he was more concerned with shutting off a bomb than he was in preventing Spider from catching short balls. He told Thomas this as they took the field following the Packer kickoff, which Herm Weiskopf had returned to the Ram 34 on a squirming, twisting run which justified his nickname of Squirmin' Herman.

"Good," Thomas said. "We want to control the ball on them."

Control the ball he did on another slow, subtle drive which used 14 plays to eat up the 65-yard road to the touchdown. This time he played on the habits and expectancies he had drilled into the Packer defense in the first drive. The running plays started the same with the same blocking patterns, then changed in mid stride. Ottum took a pitchout and began the wide sweep to his left which had gained sixteen yards to open the game, but this time Spider, after faking in as though he were going to crack back on the linebacker, whirled and had an easy blocking angle on Aldridge, the corner back, who had read sweep and started wide. Ottum cut back sharply against the grain of the pursuit and made 14 yards before he was hauled down.

Spider had caught a quick square out on Aldridge in the first drive, and he ran the same pattern three times in this drive, when Brad was throwing to another receiver or sending his backs diving into the line. With a third-and-7 situation on the Packer 24-yard line and the Ram march in dire danger of grinding to a halt, Thomas called a zig-in pattern to Spider, in which he would fake to the sideline, then cut in sharply seven yards downfield.

Aldridge took the outside fake, but his tremendous reaction allowed him to follow Spider quickly when he slanted back to the inside. If Thomas had not placed the ball perfectly, Spider might not have been able to catch it or Aldridge might have knocked it down. The play went for seven and a half yards and the first down.

Spider was hit hard just as he caught the ball, and he was slammed into the ground viciously as he went down, with Aldridge on top of him. He relaxed as he went down and the impact did not hurt him, but, as he got up, he noticed that Aldridge was still down. He paused to see if the Packer back was injured, but Aldridge climbed to his feet quickly and stared at Spider, his dark face impassive. He trotted back to the Packer defensive huddle, and Spider carefully watched him go. It seemed to him that Aldridge was fighting to avoid limping on his left leg, and Spider filed the knowledge away for future use.

Brad slammed at the Packer line with probes by Ottum, Tilson, and Werner, the big backs churning ahead powerfully for three and four yards at a crack. Steadman was alternating them, letting one of the running backs rest every third play, and the stratagem kept them relatively fresh and warm in the bitter cold. Spider wished for a moment that Gallagher could handle a wide receiver spot well enough to spell him and Gangel, but he dismissed the wish immediately. He knew Steadman would not use Gallagher unless someone were injured.

The touchdown came on first and goal from the Packer two. The big Packer defense massed to turn back the expected thrust into the line, and Brad flipped a quick sideline pass to Gangel in the corner of the end zone for the score.

The Ram defense held after yielding yardage to midfield on the next Packer drive, and once again Brad marshaled the Ram forces on a multi-play, ball-control march which produced the third Ram touchdown 28 seconds before the half, on a quarterback sneak by Brad himself. The club left the field with a 21-7 lead, but clearly in control of the game.

During the half, Berman quietly went over some minor adjustments in blocking patterns and pass routes, designed to take advantage of the anticipated changes the Packers would make to contain the short-yardage Ram attack.

His anticipation was accurate, and the Ram attack ground for another touchdown in the third period. After that, neither team could move the ball well and the Rams, with five minutes to go in the game, led 28-7. Thomas had gone all the way at quarterback, and Spider was surprised when he heard Steadman tell Frog to warm up as the Packers prepared to punt late in the game.

"Don't take any chances," Spider heard him tell Frog. "Control the ball, and take what they give you."

Frog stayed on the ground on his first two calls, and Rabbit Laguerre and Squirmin' Herman Weiskopf, the rookie running backs, bounced and scrambled for a first down. They were fresh and eager, and their bright, clean uniforms contrasted clearly with the dirty uniforms of the vets. Spider noticed that now Aldridge was limping heavily on his left leg, and he told Frog, going back to the huddle, "I can beat Aldridge deep on a slant in and corner." Aldridge would not be able to cut back to the outside off the bad leg.

Frog called the play and when Spider cut on a slant outside to the corner, he heard Aldridge gasp behind him as he looked for the ball. It floated into his hands easily, and he was all alone for sixty yards and a touchdown.

Chapter 16

THE warmth of the dressing room was a grateful relief to Spider. He had not realized how chilly it had grown when the sun slid below the edge of the stadium, nor had he realized how tired he was until the gun went off, signifying the Ram victory and the Western Conference Championship. Spider slumped wearily before his locker, trying to summon energy to start stripping off his uniform. The clubhouse was curiously quiet and subdued after the win; Spider and the other players knew that they still had two big games ahead of them before they could celebrate wholeheartedly.

The Cleveland Browns had played the Dallas Cowboys in Dallas for the Eastern Conference title, but the game started later in Dallas so both games could be on national TV, and Spider wondered what was happening in the Texas city.

He had unlaced his shoes and slipped them off and was rubbing toes, numb from cold, when Jack Oslen squatted down beside him, notebook cocked and ready.

"Back to the salt mines, eh, Spider?" he said, his spectacles glistening with condensed moisture.

"What?" Spider asked. He did not understand the writer.

"I mean back to the old three yards and a cloud of dust," Oslen said. "How many balls did you catch today?"

"I don't know," Spider said. "What difference does it make? We won."

"You put everybody in the press box to sleep doing it," Oslen said. "Has Brad's hand made it impossible for him to throw long?"

"No," Spider said. "He can throw long as well as he ever did."

"Then why did you wait until Frog came in to use the bomb?"

"It wasn't there until then," Spider said. He started to explain, but Oslen got up and hurried across the room to talk to Howard. Spider watched the tall, gangling figure retreat, and shook his head.

"What's your friend after?" Gangel asked him. He was at the next locker, and like Spider, he looked tired and battered. Even a losing Packer team managed to leave its mark on the other club.

"Don't ask me," Spider said wearily. "We win by four TDs, and to listen to him, you'd think we lost the ball game."

"Two to go," Dick said. "You think you'll make it?"

"Sometimes I wonder," Spider said. "Then I think of that

172

twenty-five gees waiting for the Super Bowl winner, and I feel fresh as a daisy."

"I know what you mean," Dick said. "What you gonna do with yours?"

"Win it first," Spider said. He finished taking off his uniform, wrapped a towel around his waist, and made his way to the shower. The shower room was crowded and steamy, and he found an open shower head and adjusted the spray until it was fine and as hot as he could stand. The steaming water eased and relaxed his aching muscles and he stood for a long time, luxuriating in the warmth.

By the time he returned to his locker, the writers had left the dressing room to file their stories. The room was quiet now as the players matter-of-factly dressed and retrieved their valuables from Bill Granholme, the equipment man, who had stored them in a locked trunk during the game.

"Nice game," Granholme said to Spider as he handed him his wallet, with the Ram championship watch from two years before stretched around it. "Nice blocking."

"Thanks," Spider said, grimacing. "I felt like a fly bouncing off a window pane trying to take the linebackers."

"You did all right," Granholme said. Ross came over to pick up his valuables and nodded at Spider. The veteran All-Pro tackle controlled his enthusiasm easily as he said "Good game, Spider." Spider could tell that the veterans still retained their antipathy toward the youth movement on the club and particularly toward him, but he did not know what he could do about it.

"Thanks, Tiny," he said. "The defense really shut them down."

173

"You got to put the points up there to win," Tiny said. "Y'all did that pretty good."

He turned from Spider and grinned at Thomas, who had just taken his watch and wallet from Granholme.

"Just like the good old days," Tiny said. "You're still the most, Brad."

"*You* could have played quarterback today," Thomas told him. "Might have set a league record for overweight quarterbacks."

Ross laughed and walked away, and Spider returned to his locker to pick up his shaving equipment in its small case. The Rams had won easily enough, he thought, but the victory did not seem to have done much to seal the breach between the veterans, and the rookies, and younger players.

On the plane back to Los Angeles, the rift, to anyone looking for it, was obvious enough. None of the older players shared a seat with any of the young lions, and the hearts games which sprang up always included members of one of the factions or the other, but never both.

Florence sat down by Spider when Gangel went back to join one of the hearts games and flipped through the duplicated copy of the game play-by-play and statistics he had brought from the press box.

"Seen these?" he asked.

"No," Spider told him. "How did we do statistically?"

"Not as well as you've been averaging lately," Florence said. "But you were playing the best defense in the league."

"They're tough," Spider said. "They don't give you anything. You've got to earn it."

"Brad had a good day," Florence said. Spider nodded and

174

Florence looked at him inquisitively. "Any big difference when he's in there instead of Howard?"

"Not really," Spider said. "The game plan is the same for both of them. The ready list doesn't change." The ready list was the twenty or thirty plays of the Ram arsenal of two or three hundred that the coaches selected to concentrate on for a specific game.

"How about the bomb in the fourth period when Frog came in?"

"That wasn't in the game plan," Spider said. "Aldridge had a bad knee, and we knew he wouldn't be able to take me deep, so we took a shot at it."

Florence nodded.

"Yeah," he said. "I figured something was wrong with him. But I didn't notice him limping earlier. When did he hurt his knee?"

"Sometime in the first half," Spider said. He made an effort to remember precisely when it was that he had first noticed Aldridge trying to hide his limp, and although he could remember watching the Green Bay back forcing himself to return to his defensive huddle as though nothing were wrong with him, he could not remember how deep in the half it had been. "I think it was the second quarter," he said.

"Oh?" said Florence, raising his eyebrows and looking startled. It was one of his most-used expressions and it made Spider smile. Florence looked like a startled middle-aged faun. "He played most of the game on a flat wheel?"

"It didn't seem to bother him much," Spider said. "Then we were using short patterns and controlling the ball, and he didn't have to take me deep on any long patterns."

"Still, I would think that knowing he had lost some of his

speed, you might suggest throwing over him," Florence said.

"You don't suggest plays to Brad," Spider said, grinning. "Or not often, anyway. He runs the huddle. He listens to you, but he sticks pretty close to the game plan, especially when it's working as well as it did today."

"I see," Florence said, knitting his brows in thought. "So you waited until Frog came in to tell him about it. Is that right?"

"Not exactly," Spider said. "You trying to make it sound like I saved this one for Frog?"

"No, no!" Florence said, holding up both hands in protest. "Nothing like that. I just meant . . . well, after all . . ."

"We were going all right," Spider said. "I guess I really forgot about it, Mal. We weren't using any deep patterns, and Aldridge has lots of moxie. He didn't start to show the limp much until the fourth quarter. Then, I guess, when it got real cold, the knee started to stiffen up and the limp got worse, and I thought about it. That was just about the time Frog came in; I told him I could beat Aldridge deep, and we took a shot at it."

"Would you have done the same with Brad in the game?"

Spider thought a moment. He had not considered his motives in giving Frog the advice during the game. It was something you did, whether the quarterback was Thomas or Howard, although Frog, because of his relative inexperience as the number one, was more apt to listen than Brad. Brad might listen, but he would file the information away to use when he needed it most. He had usually made up his mind what his play call would be while the team was coming back to the huddle, so that he was not likely to change it for a whim.

"Well?" Florence said and Spider realized that he had been quiet for several moments thinking about the question.

"Sure," he said. He explained to Florence the difference in the two quarterbacks' reactions to information from players on the field. "So," he wound up, "I probably would have told Brad what I told Frog, but that doesn't mean he would have called it on the next play, or during the game, for that matter. It would depend upon how badly he thought we needed it."

"But the play got a touchdown," Mal said. "I should think you could use a touchdown any time you can get one."

"That's true enough," Spider explained patiently. "But suppose I had told Brad about it earlier in the game. Aldridge was still moving pretty good, and for all I knew, he might have been trying to sucker me. You know, give me the limp-leg bit looking for the long one, then pick it off."

Florence thought about that for a few moments. He scratched his head and still looked puzzled.

"So?" he said. "Didn't the same thing go when you told Frog about it?"

"I don't think so," Spider said. "There were about five minutes to play, we were leading by three touchdowns, and Frog throws the ball a mile. So if Aldridge was asking for the long one to intercept it, it would have been as good as a long punt, anyway. The Packers would have been way down deep in their own territory needing three touchdowns and a field goal to win, and they would have been dead, figuring the way our defense was going. They needed a blocked punt, a short interception, an on-side kick and lots of luck. Aldridge wouldn't be looking to kid anyone that far gone in the game."

"I see," Florence said. He grinned shamefacedly. "At least, I think I see. Thanks anyway, Spider. Sometimes this game gets pretty complicated for us writers."

"I wish all of them understood it as well as you do," Spider said, and meant it. "Or would ask questions about the things they don't understand."

"Well," Florence said. "Well. I guess I better go attack the typewriter. Thanks again."

Surprisingly, there was a small crowd awaiting them at the Los Angeles airport when the plane dropped down to its feathery landing at nine in the evening. The team had taken the victory with aplomb and little celebration, and it had not occurred to Spider until he came to the door of the plane and looked out at the gathering cheering the team, that most of the TV sets in Los Angeles had been tuned to Milwaukee.

The fans cheered when they recognized him, and he waved. He went down the steps and as he came closer to the crowd, he saw a few hand scrawled placards being waved over their heads. In the dim light, it was hard to read them, but he finally made out a sign which said, "With Leggett and Howard, We Will Go Forward!" Although he could not say much for the rhyme, he grinned to himself at the sentiment.

"BRAD'S THE LAD!!!" another sign read. It was being waved angrily by a middle-aged man who hopped up and down in his excitement. As Spider made his way into the terminal, he heard conflicting chants of "We want Howard!" and "We want Thomas!" A scuffle broke out as he went through the door into the terminal, and he was glad to be out of sight of the fans, as much as he appreciated them.

"Good to be back," Thomas said at his right, and he looked up at the quarterback and nodded.

178

"I hope they like us just as well next Sunday night," he said.

"The Cowboys are tough," Brad said. "Real tough."

"Hey," Spider said, excited. "The Cowboys won? Where did you hear that?"

"The captain told me while we were getting off the plane," Brad said. "They waxed the Browns. He thought it was 52-14."

Spider whistled softly.

"They must have been hot," he said. "You seen them play at all this year?" The Cowboys were in the Eastern Conference, and the Rams had not played their division. Each team in the National Football League played every team in its own division twice, every team in the other division in its conference once, and every team in one division from the other conference once. This season, the Rams had not played the Eastern Division the Cowboys belonged to.

"No," Brad said. "I'll see a lot of them on film this week, though. We'll have three of their games to look at, and we'll have to set up the offense from scratch, I guess. We played them last year, but I guess they have changed a lot."

They had reached the main part of the terminal, and Spider picked up his bag and made his way out toward the parking lot. Thomas walked with him a little way.

"Need a ride?" he asked casually, and Spider shook his head.

"I left my car here," he said. "I hope it's still here."

"Maybe without any wheels," Thomas said and laughed. "Good night, Spider. Good game."

He turned to go, and Spider said, "Same to you, Brad. You called a beauty."

179

"Good game plan," Brad said. "The coaching staff did a job."

He waved and strode away, and Spider went to look for his car. He found it intact and only a little reluctant to start after sitting for four days.

After he finally got the motor turning over smoothly, he switched on the radio and started the long drive to Long Beach. Gangel had brought his own car, so Spider was alone, and he relished the solitude.

He thought about the conversation with Brad Thomas and was surprised to find that there had been no bitterness in it. He had felt that he and Thomas were, at best, in a state of armed truce, but Thomas had been friendly and warm.

He felt guilty about being disloyal to Howard, but he knew, going over the game in his mind, that Brad's direction had been flawless.

Howard could have done as well, he thought. Probably better.

But he was not sure.

Chapter 17

THE game for the National Football League Championship and a berth in the Super Bowl against the champion of the American Football League, was to be played in Dallas. The Rams had been host the year before, and the home team alternated between the Eastern and Western Conferences.

So the Rams spent only one day in Los Angeles before flying to Dallas. Although Steadman was not much in favor of going to Dallas so early, it was customary for the two teams in the championship game to arrive as early as possible, and the weather forecast for Dallas was good.

They stayed at the Holiday Central Motel, a big, sprawling two-story structure not far from downtown Dallas and a twenty-minute ride from the Cotton Bowl, where the game would be played.

The club worked on a high-school field in preparation for the game and, to Spider's relief, the weather was crisp but bright and sunny, with the same long-range forecast for the game day.

In the intensity of the preparation for the game, the split in the team personnel was almost forgotten. None of the players, veteran or new, had time to pursue anything other than study of the Dallas offense and defense; the daily practice was preceded and followed, after dinner, by team meetings. Early in the week, they made exhaustive study of the Cowboy film, and Spider concentrated on the defensive back who would be covering him.

His name was Jap Cartwright, and he had been an all-conference defensive back from his second season in the league on. He was now in his fifth season, and Spider was impressed when he watched him in action.

Cartwright was not a big man. The program showed him six feet tall, weighing 185 pounds, which made him a little heavier than Spider. However, he was one of the few players Spider had ever faced who would be able to match his speed. Cartwright had been a sprint champion in college, and unlike many sprinters, he had extraordinary lateral mobility as well as good top speed. He had an uncanny faculty for anticipating plays, and time and again Spider saw him, in the film, apparently diagnose a pattern ahead of time and ignore fakes to go to the target point and either break up the pass or intercept it.

"He doesn't have many interceptions," Dickey, the Ram end coach, pointed out. "But interceptions aren't the mark of

182

a great defensive back, Spider. They are the mark of a back who gambles. Check the touchdown passes caught against Cartwright. One. That's the criterion. Another mark of the great defensive back is the respect the other teams show him. If you noticed in the film, not many clubs try to throw into his area."

"Sounds like a long afternoon for me," Spider said apprehensively.

"Maybe not," Dickey said. "We'll see what we can work out."

The Dallas defense, as it was explained by Berman, was complex and difficult, hard to read, and hard to adjust to. Coach Tom Landry, the scholarly head coach of the Cowboys, was recognized as one of the defensive geniuses of football, and he had, over a period of years, assembled precisely the kind of personnel he needed for his carefully planned defensive stratagems. The Cowboys used a keying defense, one in which each member of the defensive squad reacted to specific actions of a player on the opposite team, and it was unnatural for a player, at first. After the keys had been learned, however, the defense was as difficult to penetrate as any in football.

The offense Steadman put in for the championship game was designed to negate the keys of the Cowboy defenders, and it involved rather subtle changes in blocking assignments and pass patterns. The changes were not extensive; Steadman did not have time to put in sweeping changes in the short week he had to get the club ready for the game.

To Spider's dismay, he found that he would be used far more as a decoy than as a primary target in the Ram passing offense.

183

"We have to figure that they are very much aware of you," Dickey explained to him. "So they'll be keying on you in most passing situations. If we can convince them that you are the primary receiver, we may be able to get them off balance. So we'll be using you more to clear an area than to catch a pass. That means you'll have to run your fakes just as hard as ever, knowing that, in all likelihood, you won't be getting the pass."

"I see," Spider said.

"If they adjust at the half, then we can go back to the old patterns," Dickey said. "If that happens, Brad will be hitting you."

Spider worked doggedly during the week learning the variations on the theme of the Ram pass offense. He was not happy at the role he would have to play, but he realized it was for the good of the team, and he was resigned to it. With his role reduced to decoy, most of the Ram pass attack would be directed toward Gangel and to backs coming out of the backfield.

In order to preserve the element of surprise in the offense, Steadman ordered secret practices, and had the practice field surrounded with a high canvas fence to prevent the curious from watching. At mid-week, an unauthorized observer was discovered in a tree overlooking the field and hauled down ingloriously, but he proved to be only an over-enthusiastic Ram fan who had made the trip from Los Angeles and was determined to watch his club workout.

The Los Angeles sports writers were understandably annoyed when Steadman decreed that the ban held for them, as well as for everyone else not directly connected with the team, but they could do nothing about it except complain.

"What the dickens are you guys putting in?" Oslen asked Spider once in the lobby of the motel. "The single wing?"

"Something like that," Spider said innocently. He did not really understand why Steadman had closed the practices. Most sportswriters would not recognize the small changes in the offense, anyway.

Although the ill feeling between the two factions on the team had receded on the squad itself, the debate about the relative merits of Howard and Thomas went on in the Los Angeles papers.

Oslen still inveighed against Steadman for going back to Brad Thomas, despite the success Frog Howard had had leading the team. Although he had a hard time discovering anything to criticize about Thomas's game against the Packers, he did point out, gleefully, that Howard had been able to penetrate the supposedly impregnable deep defense of Green Bay with the bomb to Spider in the closing minutes.

"To this writer," he wound up, "this play sums up the difference in the two quarterbacks. Thomas is a fine, sound quarterback who executes a game plan errorlessly, but Howard can do everything Thomas can, and he combines it with a touch of genius."

Florence, recounting the background of the long pass as he had gotten it from Spider on the plane, remained undecided, but seemed to lean toward Frog, too.

"Certainly, Leggett did not consciously keep the information about Aldridge's lame knee from Thomas," he wrote. "But it is fair to assume that subconsciously he remembered the lack of confidence Thomas had shown in him in previous games and to suppose that had Howard been in the game earlier, Leggett would have used the information earlier. He

185

knew how Howard would react; he was not sure how Thomas would. In a game as important as a championship game, it might be wise to use all the information available all the time."

Spider tried to explain to Brad what he had said to Florence to prompt the story, but Brad grinned and slapped him on the shoulder.

"Don't worry about it," he said. "Matter of fact, you're right. And I know you would have given me the same tip if I had been in, and I know I wouldn't have been as apt to act on it. Forget it."

By the time the club had finished the final long workout on Friday afternoon, the new offense was working smoothly, and the slight changes in assignments no longer gave pause to the players. In practice, Thomas and Howard had thrown to Spider as often as they had to the other receivers, even though his role was still that of a decoy. Although the man in the tree had proved to be an innocent observer, Steadman did not want to take a chance that there were Dallas spies hidden in the woodwork.

The Saturday morning workout was open to the public, and none of the offensive or defensive plays were rehearsed. Steadman worked the special teams on punts, and kickoffs, and kick returns. Spider and Gangel worked with the other receivers running meaningless patterns while Thomas, Howard, and Axthelm took turns throwing to them. They tried to set a record for patterns run without dropping the ball, but fell far short of the mark set several years before by Lyman and Terry. The two All-Pros had once gone through three practice sessions before either of them dropped a ball or the quarterbacks put one where they could not catch it.

186

They went through the Saturday practice flawlessly, but they knew that it did not count in this particular esoteric club record. Only regular workouts could be counted.

The final team meeting was on Saturday night, after dinner, and it was a short one.

"There's nothing else I can tell you to help you prepare," Steadman said. "If you don't know it now, you haven't got time to learn it. I think we have a good game plan on offense and defense, but it will have to be perfectly executed. The Cowboys don't make mistakes, and they capitalize on the other team's. I think we can beat them, but it will take an all-out game."

He paused for a few moments, his massive face solemn.

"I haven't said anything about this up until now," he said slowly. "I may be wrong to say anything, but I think not. I don't have to tell you that there has been a growing division on this team in the last few weeks. You know it a lot better than I do. I don't know who is at fault or if any one player or group of players is at fault. I do know that whatever the reason and however the club is split, it must stop once we take the field. You can't beat Dallas or any other good team if the whole team is not involved as a team. If you have differences, forget them. If you hate someone on this club, forget that. If you have any grudge, if you have any prejudice, forget it. Think of one thing. Beating Dallas."

He was quiet again, thinking, then shook his head.

"That's all," he said. "I don't have anything else to tell you."

They trooped out of the room silently, avoiding looking at each other, and Spider wondered if Steadman blamed him personally for the division on the team.

"Looks like he's closing the gate after the horse got out," Gangel said as they walked down the long corridor to their room. "I think most of the antagonism has died out, don't you?"

"I guess so," Spider said, doubtfully. "At least we've been so busy this week, I haven't noticed any. But I haven't noticed any of the veterans breaking their backs to be friendly, either."

"Thomas seems friendly enough," Gangel said.

"He's different," Spider said. "Maybe it's because he's a team captain as well as quarterback."

"Maybe so," Gangel said. "And maybe it's because he knows he has to depend on all of us to protect him. He doesn't want anyone opening the gates on him."

Spider was shocked as he looked at Gangel.

"No one would do that anyway," he said. "Even when I was mad at him, I never thought of not blocking for him."

"I was kidding," Gangel said, and laughed. "Neither did I."

Spider had been afraid that he would be unable to sleep the night before the game, but he dropped off the moment his head hit the pillow, even before Gangel's stentorian snores disturbed the quiet. Most nights Gangel beat him to sleep, and he had to cover his head with a pillow to muffle the sound of his roommate's snores.

He awoke feeling strong and fresh and ready for the trials of the day. He had an unreasonable feeling of optimism, and he told Gangel, as they dressed, "This one's ours, Dick. I got a feeling."

"I got one, too," Gangel said sourly. "I feel like I just swallowed a bucket of flying worms."

"You'll feel better after the pre-game meal," Spider said

cheerfully. He was ravenously hungry himself, and he always ate a big steak, plus eggs, milk, orange juice, toast and coffee before a game. Gangel rarely had more than a poached egg and sometimes had trouble keeping that down.

"I guess you'll eat like a horse as usual," Gangel said. "I don't know where a guy your size puts everything."

"High power engine needs lots of fuel," Spider said. "Hurry up. I'm starving."

The dressing room in the Cotton Bowl was small and crowded with narrow stalls for the players' uniforms, and Spider, as he changed into his uniform, wondered again why a stadium as big and impressive as this one did not provide better locker rooms for the teams. He did not worry about that for long, though.

Steadman glanced at his wirst watch and said, "Let's go out for the warm-up. Come on."

The team walked down a long ramp that opened into one end zone of the big bowl, and, as they took the field to start calisthenics, Spider saw that the seats were already well filled, although it was almost an hour before game time. The feeling of euphoria which had possessed him since he had awakened was replaced, momentarily, by a hollow emptiness which nauseated him for breath, then was gone.

Mike Brawley, the big middle linebacker who was captain of the defense, led them briskly through the calisthenics, and then the club broke up into smaller groups. Spider took his place in the line of receivers running patterns for the quarterbacks and bounced nervously as he waited his turn. When it came, Thomas indicated with a twitch of his hand that he wanted him to run a deep fly pattern, and Spider raced downfield and caught the perfect pass over his shoul-

189

der, easily. The pattern had taken him into the Cowboy end of the field, and he was aware of the scrutiny of the Dallas players as he trotted back.

Thomas and Howard threw him several more deep passes into the Dallas area during the warm-up, and Spider grinned to himself. It did not hurt to start psyching the other club early; all of the passes were dead on target, and he took all of them casually, as if he could not conceive of missing one.

When they left the field before the kickoff, Spider tried to pick out Cartwright, the defensive back who would take him and finally discovered him working on a last back-up drill. He was a sturdy, tough looking man, and Spider was impressed with the agility with which he changed direction, sprinted and moved to the ball in the drill.

The dressing room was quiet as the team made the final preparations for the game, putting pads under the jerseys, tightening shoelaces and putting charcoal under their eyes to cut the glare of the bright sun.

Spider could feel the tension building in him now, and he was as quiet as the others. It was with a feeling of relief that he heard an official knock on the door, stick his head in, and say, "On the field, Rams!"

Chapter 18

I T WAS late in the second period before Spider caught his first pass. The game was tied, 14-14, and the Ram touchdowns had come on a swing pass to Bob Ottum from the Cowboy 22-yard line, with Ottum trailing into an area Spider had cleared by taking the corner back deep with him while the tight end occupied the safety, leaving the corner linebacker the unenviable task of trying to cope with the fleet Ottum man-for-man.

The other Ram touchdown was the result of a slithering, stop-and-go kickoff return by Rabbit Laguerre after the Cowboys had gone ahead 14-7. Laguerre caught the ball five yards deep in the end zone, fumbled, then picked it up and to the horror of the Rams on the sideline, elected to try to run it out.

He met the lead defender in the Cowboy defense head on at the 15-yard line and bounced back what seemed to Spider like five yards. He landed running and the second wave converged on him so that, for a moment, he was lost to sight from the sideline. When Spider found him again, the big youngster was at the far sidelne, turning up field. He had retreated to the Ram 10-yard line tryng to find running room, and three Cowboys seemed to have him pinned to the sideline, but he cut back and suddenly found a corridor of blockers. The rest of the run was easy.

The Rams had stopped the Cowboys cold on the ensuing kickoff, and now Spider, running another decoy pattern, turned back toward the line of scrimmage and saw Thomas scrambling away from a blitz. He curled back to the line, and yelled, and Brad lofted him a short pass. As he turned, he was hit hard by Cartwright, and the play gained four yards.

Thomas went back to the game plan, hit Werner with a flare pass, then found Gangel on a quick slant in to put the ball at midfield. Three plays later, Rocky Stebbins banged a long high kick through the goal for a 47-yard field goal, and the Rams led, 17-14. It was still 17-14 at the half.

There were few adjustments made during the half. The Ram passing attack, while it had not been overpowering, had been good enough, and Berman was reluctant to return to the old patterns.

"If they change their coverage," he said, "we'll pick it up in the first couple of series, then we can make the adjustment. But I don't think they will."

He glanced at Spider. "Nice job, Leggett," he said. "Keep running your fakes out hard."

"Sure," Spider said. Running deep fakes over and over again had left him leg weary by the end of the first half, but the half-time rest refreshed him, and he felt ready to go another half at top speed. He could not help hoping that the Cowboy pass defense would be changed enough for him to become a primary target a few times in the last two quarters.

The Cowboy kickoff was a floater deep to the Ram goal line. The ball sailed and shifted like a knuckle ball, and watching it drop, Spider tried to send Laguerre a mental message to let it go and down it in the end zone. But Rabbit circled under the ball hesitantly for what seemed to be an hour, dived at it desperately at the last moment, then scrambled after it into the end zone on his hands and knees. Just before he reached it, most of the Cowboy kickoff team fell on Laguerre and the ball, and seconds later, the official on the scene raised both arms. Suddenly the Cowboys were ahead.

"Shake it off," Spider said as Laguerre hobbled to the sideline. Rabbit looked at him dazedly and started to sit down.

"You're on again," Granholme said to him. "They're kicking off."

This time the kickoff sailed into the end zone and the Rams went into action on their own 20-yard line. Brad tried two running plays which were stopped dead, then threw a pass to Werner, but the Cowboy linebacker batted it away, and Boomer Terrell went in to punt.

For the rest of the third period and into the fourth, it was

Terrell's long high punts which saved the Rams from disaster. The Cowboy defense, perfectly keyed, stopped both the Ram running and passing attack cold, and the Dallas attack moved the ball slowly but steadily. Twice they missed long field goals; when they neared the Ram goal line, the Los Angeles defense stiffened.

The Rams changed the keys, but the Cowboys adjusted quickly and well, and Spider, now a primary pass target as often as not, found that Cartwright was just as tough as he had looked in the movies. With uncanny prescience, the Dallas defense seemed to double him every time Brad called his pattern. As the fourth quarter wore on with the score still 21-17, Dallas, he began to despair.

Despite the difficulties the Ram offense was encountering, Thomas seemed as cool and confident as ever as he called the plays. When the Ram defense was on the field—which seemed to be most of the time—he conferred calmly with the scouts in the press box and translated their suggestions into action when he returned to the field. But nothing was working, and to Spider, it seemed that the Ram hopes for an NFL Championship and a Super Bowl victory were disappearing.

With four minutes and a few seconds left to play, the Cowboys punted deep to the Ram 4-yard line, and Laguerre, wisely, signaled for a fair catch, then stepped aside to let the ball go into the end zone. But it took a freak bounce and died, and the Rams came on the field to start what would most likely be their last chance to score with the ball on the six.

As they kneeled in the huddle, Spider expected to hear Thomas call for a long pass. Instead, Brad glanced around the group of intent faces calmly and said, matter-of-factly, "Now we have to move. Let's make everything sure."

He called a quick trap with Tilson carrying the ball, and the big Negro fullback sliced into a quick hole created when Harv Grut smashed a Cowboy tackle out of the way with a driving trap block.

Ottum picked up another five yards behind a sure block by Hoy Yuen, the veteran Hawaiian tackle, and it was third and 1 at the Ram 15-yard line. Thomas called a play action pass, sent Tilson into the line again, and flipped the ball over the middle to Slats Shrake, the veteran tight end, for seven yards and the first down.

The huddle was quiet and determined now, and somehow Spider could feel the determination and the pride of the veteran Ram starters. There were no pep talks and Thomas's voice was unemotional as he called the plays, but the plays went with snap and power and, as the ball moved slowly toward the Cowboy goal line, Spider suddenly realized that Thomas was going almost entirely with his veterans. On the key plays, he called a hole over a veteran offensive lineman. Grut and Nathan, the guards, did yeoman service handling the powerful Cowboy tackles, and Yuen and DeFord, the big offensive tackles, kept the Cowboy defensive ends off Thomas when he called a pass.

The pass patterns went to Shrake and the backs, all of them veterans, and they ran the patterns impeccably and caught the ball under pressure, over and over. The clock was moving, but Thomas seemed not to be aware of it. The Rams had two time-outs left, and he did not use either of them until well after the two-minute warning had been given to the benches.

Caught up in the deep determination of the team, Spider carried out his assignments fiercely, running his fakes at top speed, blocking violently when he was called upon to and praying desperately that nothing would go wrong.

He could feel the enormous pressure building as the clock moved, and the game came closer to being irrevocably lost. Thomas could not settle for moving into field goal range and depending on Stebbins to save the day; the Rams trailed by four points, and a field goal would be useless.

Only once had Brad called a pass to Spider by the time the Rams reached the Cowboy 35-yard line with 45 seconds left on the clock. The pass had been a quick squareout to the sideline, designed to stop the clock by being thrown incomplete if Spider were covered, or give Spider the opportunity to stop it by stepping out of bounds if he caught the ball.

Cartwright was dogging Spider closely, and Brad threw the ball away, stopping the clock. As Spider returned to the huddle, Brad said, "He's up tight, Spider. Can you beat him deep?"

Spider started to say "Yes" without thinking, then checked himself. On the deep fakes he had run, he had been surprised at how well Cartwright went with him on man-to-man coverage and how quickly he was picked up in a deep zone. The game had been frustrating for him in more ways than one, and he was tempted to say that he could take Cartwright, but he didn't.

"He gets back fast," he said. "And most of the time, they're zoning me deep."

Thomas nodded and went back to the huddle to call another pass to a trailing back. This time Werner caught the ball and gained six hard yards as Cowboy tacklers swarmed over him.

From the Dallas 35-yard line, Thomas called two plays in the huddle. The first was another sideline to Spider and this time he caught the ball just as he made his cut and just as Cartwright hit him, and he dragged the defender over the sideline to stop the clock.

With the clock stopped, the club huddled again instead of using the second call. Thomas called the play unemotionally and precisely, and Spider was surprised to hear that it was a zig-in to him. If he caught the ball, he would not be near the sideline and could not stop the clock.

When he made his fake to the sideline, Cartwright over-reacted and as Spider turned in, the ball was in his hands, and he ran for fourteen yards before the safeties converged on him. As he went down, he could hear Brad yelling "Time, time!"

The two plays had gained twenty yards, and the ball was on the Dallas 15-yard line with 34 seconds on the clock as Brad trotted to the sideline to talk to Steadman and Berman.

As he waited for the time-out to end, Spider realized how apt Brad's call had been. The Cowboys would not be looking for any pattern to the inside, since a pass completed there would almost certainly not go all the way, and any completed pass would use up precious time, since it would not stop the clock. Brad had bought 14 precious yards on the calculated gamble.

Thomas came back from the sideline, and Spider searched his face as he approached. If Brad felt any of the tremendous pressure, he did not show it. His face was serene and confident, and his voice was certain as he called two plays in the huddle. Both were pass plays, but neither was to Spider or Dick. The first was a wide flair to Ottum behind the line. If it worked, he would be able to get out of bounds and if not, the odds against an interception were good, and Brad would have the safe sideline to throw the ball into and stop the clock.

The pass was good, and Ottum gained four yards before he was forced out of bounds. Spider had run a short slant in, a pattern designed to keep him close to the line of scrimmage so that he could race back into position and line up for the next play with a minimum loss of time.

The next play was a daring call, a halfback option with Werner running to his left and throwing the ball to Spider if Spider was clear, or keeping it for a sweep if he was not. Spider had to fake a block, then sift into the secondary, and he made the block as genuine as he could without losing his feet. When he released, he was open for a moment and Werner threw the ball low and behind Spider. He leaned back, and scooped it up, and dived for the sideline, but did not quite make it.

"Time, time!" Brad yelled as Spider got to his feet. He looked up at the clock and saw that only 11 seconds were left in the game. The ball was now on the Cowboy 6-yard line.

Time stretched out endlessly while Brad ambled back to the Ram bench to consult with Steadman and Berman. Spider had not noticed that the air had turned chilly as the sun went down, but now he shivered as he waited for Thomas to come back and the time-out to end. He figured that there would be time for two or three pass plays or a pass play and a running play. There would be no more time-outs for the Rams. They were used up.

Thomas came back as imperturbable as ever and called a quick slant out to Spider at the sideline. The pattern called for Spider to take two steps across the line, then cut to the sideline immediately. It would be a difficult pass to complete because the angle was a bad one for the quarterback, but Thomas called it confidently.

Spread wide to the left, Spider tried to give the impression that he was just going through the motions, but he felt tense and keyed up. At the snap signal, he took two quick steps, slanted to the outside and looked over his left shoulder just as the ball reached him. He caught it and turned up field, and Cartwright was there. He slanted back out again, and this time his desperate lunge took him over the sideline and stopped the clock. When he got to his feet, Brad was checking with the timekeeper to make sure how many seconds were left.

In the huddle, he said, "Four seconds. We can't take a chance on two plays. This is it." He called the play quietly and the team came out quickly. Spider lined up tight on this play, and the corner back moved in with him. Spider moved three yards wide to a flexed position, and Cartwright moved with him.

He heard Brad yell "Set!" and on the "Hup!" that followed, he drove at Cartwright's knees and got a piece of the back, enough to slow him down. He was on his face on the ground, and he listened and heard a deep stillness and jumped to his feet and howled.

The call had been a quarterback sneak, and when Spider reached his feet, he saw an official with both hands in the air signaling touchdown, and he yelled again and wrapped his arms around DeFord, the big tackle.

The extra point was good, and the game was over, and Spider, turning wearily from the sideline to walk across the field and up the ramp to the dressing room, suddenly felt as though he could not take another step. His feet dragged, and he found it difficult to put one foot in front of the other. The tremendous emotional drain had left him completely used up.

By the time he reached the small, crowded dressing room, he had revived. This time the club was whooping and shouting with glee and Spider joined the rest of them. He found himself pouring champagne on the head of Tiny Ross, and the big tackle lifted him bodily and swung him around.

"How sweet it is!" Tiny yelled, swinging Spider around as easily as if he had been a rag doll. "One more and how sweet it is!"

He put Spider down, and engulfed his hand in an enormous paw, and shook it violently.

"You done well, son," he hollered. "You done real well!"

Spider grinned at him and all the tiredness left him and he felt as light as a cloud. He made his way to his locker through a light rain of champagne, and sat down and was surprised to find, all at once, that he was close to tears.

Steadman stood in the middle of the small room and yelled for quiet, and slowly the bedlam died down. The massive coach was wet from champagne and from having been pushed under a shower, but he did not seem to mind.

"You played like champions," he said. "All of you. Like a championship team. The writers are coming in in a minute, and before you say anything to any of them, I want you to remember, you *are* a team. A great team."

They cheered him lustily and Steadman nodded to the policeman on the door, and he opened it a crack. A writer thrust a press pass into the crack, and the policeman let him in, and in five minutes the small room was packed with sportswriters, TV interviewers, cameramen, and radio interviewers wandering about with tape recorders over their shoulders.

Spider watched them come, then undressed hurriedly and went in to the showers. Somehow, this was a victory he wanted to relish a while before he talked about it.

Chapter 19

THE Super Bowl game was schemuled in the Orange Bowl for two weeks after the NFL and AFL wind-ups in Miami, so Steadman gave the club four days off before taking them to Miami. The four-day rest was a welcome one for Spider and the rest of the players; their game with San Diego, the team which had won the AFL title, would be their 23rd since the beginning of the exhibition season back in early August.

Spider spent the four-day respite relaxing and trying to forget football, but he had no luck in the latter. The Los Angeles newspapers, and radio and TV stations were busily engaged in rehashing the victory over Dallas and looking forward to the game against San Diego. All of them pointed out the irony of two southern California football teams playing for the World Championship in Florida, and most of them criticized Commissioner Pete Rozelle for the unfortunate circumstance, but the game had been scheduled for over a year.

Spider himself would have preferred to play in the friendly confines of Memorial Coliseum, but the Super Bowl had been played in Miami every year except the first, when the Green Bay Packers had demolished the Kansas City Chiefs in the Coliseum. The games had grown steadily closer as the younger league improved, but no NFL team had ever lost. Spider was grimly determined not to be a member of the first losing team from the senior league.

To his surprise, most of the Los Angeles writers were severely critical of Brad Thomas after the victory over Dallas. Instead of dwelling on the brilliant series of plays he had called under the tremendous pressure of dwindling time to get the Rams their game-winning touchdown, they deplored what they chose to call his lack of imagination earlier. Oslen, of course, was the most critical.

"John Steadman seems to be determined to live or die with Brad Thomas," Oslen wrote. "He came within seconds of dying against Dallas, and unless he can overcome his prejudice against Frog Howard, he may not survive against the San Diego Chargers. For the first time since the Super Bowl began, the AFL entry is at least as good and quite possibly, better than the champion of the NFL. Of the uninspired performance Thomas gave against the Cowboys, it must be said that, if he is still the Ram quarterback in Miami, the Chargers will have to be favored. With Howard in, the Rams seem to have a narrow edge."

Bob Oates, the scholarly pro writer for the *Herald Exami-*

ner, was not as forthright as Oslen, but he, too, felt that Howard might have done a better job than Thomas against the Cowboys.

"In evaluating the efficiency of Thomas against the Cowboys," he wrote, "you must realize that the Dallas defense is probably the best in football, especially against the pass. Thomas attacked it scientifically and well with the tools at his disposal."

Spider nodded to himself as he read the story. Oates did not realize just how well Thomas had used his tools.

"However," Oates went on, "there is a point in every game where a quarterback must depend upon art, not science. He must have a flair for the unexpected if he is to be a really great quarterback. For example, when Bart Starr was the quarterback of the Green Bay Packers, he was incomparable as a technician and strategist. He almost never made a mistake. But the key to his greatness was his readiness to stray from the game plan now and then with a totally unexpected call. Often, when the Packers found themselves with third down and 2 or 3 yards to go around midfield, Starr would call a play action pass, sending his fullback into the line and throwing to a halfback or an end. Sometimes he failed, but more often the pass went for a long gain or a touchdown. It was the kind of play Frog Howard might call, but not the kind that Brad Thomas would. Thomas, over the years, seems to have become too conservative. And conservative football will not beat a team as explosive as the San Diego Chargers."

One night during the four-day hiatus, Spider had dinner with Howard, Gangel, and Rabbit Laguerre. They ate at The Bat Rack, a big, comfortable restaurant in Santa Monica run by Johnny Sproutt, an inveterate pro-football fan who had been a particular admirer of Norman Van Brocklin when the Dutchman quarterbacked the Rams, and later the Philadelphia Eagles. Sproutt was a small, cheerful man with a gravelly voice, and his restaurant served exceptionally good, and exceptionally big steaks.

"Hi, little buddy," he croaked to Spider when he entered the restaurant. "How you hittin' 'em?"

"I don't figure to play any golf for a while yet," Spider said, laughing. Sproutt was a good golfer who played almost every day of the year. "We still got the Chargers coming up."

"You ain't worried about them bums," Johnny said scornfully. "I figure you win that one three touchdowns, anyway."

"I hope you're right," Spider said. "They're tough."

"You played the tough ones already," Sproutt said. "The Packers and the Cowboys. These guys play in the Mickey Mouse league."

"Not any more," Spider said. "Maybe once. Not now."

"You'll kill 'em," Johnny said confidently. "Your buddies are back in the back room. You gonna eat a steak?"

"Sure," Spider said. "A big one."

"I'll pick it out, little buddy," Johnny said. "See you later."

The other three players were already seated at a corner booth in the big main dining room, which was dominated by a wall-size mural of Yankee Stadium. They had not ordered yet, but all of them were having steak.

Spider answered their greetings quietly, and sat down on the comfortable leather banquette, and stretched luxuriously. He laughed and said, "Seems funny not to think about practice tomorrow. I feel like I been working out every day for the last twenty years."

206

"Won't be long," Gangel said. "We leave for Miami tomorrow, and the grind starts all over."

"Look at it this way," Howard said, grinning. "For the next ten days, we're working for fifteen hundred bucks a day."

"If we win," Laguerre said. The big rookie halfback rapped his knuckles on the table. "Don't count the money now, Frog."

Frog shrugged and knocked wood.

"We'll win," he said. "We got to."

"If we don't, we'll blow the whole season," Spider said seriously. "The only thing anyone will ever remember about this Ram team is that it was the first NFL team ever to lose a Super Bowl to the AFL. They'll forget everything else we accomplished—conference championship, NFL championship, and all the rest."

"That's right," Gangel said. He glanced around the dining room carefully and lowered his voice. "One thing bothers me," he went on. "One big thing."

"What's that?" Laguerre asked, automatically lowering his voice in response to Gangel's conspiratorial tone.

"I don't want to sound like I'm griping or anything like that," Gangel said, his thin face serious. "But I figure we got to be more of a hell-for-leather club than we were against Dallas, and I don't think Brad's that kind of a quarterback. He sure played it close to his vest against the Cowboys."

The words came out in a rush, and he leaned back and looked at the other three players a little defiantly, as if he were afraid he would be chastised for being critical of Thomas.

They were silent for a minute or so, thinking of what he had said, then Howard shook his head.

"I know that's what some of the papers have been saying, Dick," he said. "But I don't think anyone could have done any better than Brad did in that game. Or as well."

"He forgot the bomb," Gangel cried. "Just plain forgot it. And look how many times you hit it to me and to Spider."

"Another thing," Laguerre said, his young face flushing. "Seems to me the only thing he could think of there at the end was to go with the veterans, the guys he's used to. How about using some of the young guys, too?"

Howard started to answer, but Spider cut in on him.

"I learned something in that game," he said. "A couple of things. First, with apologies to Frog here, I found out just exactly why Brad Thomas is the number one quarterback on this club and probably the number one in the league."

"Don't apologize to me," Frog said. "I've already told you how I feel about Brad."

"I'm not saying that Frog couldn't have got that last touchdown," Spider went on. "Maybe he could. But a funny thing happened in the huddle during that drive. I don't know if Dick felt it, but I did. We hadn't been moving the ball and when we went out, with time almost gone, I know I thought we were dead. But after the first couple of calls, somehow or other, I knew that we would score and win the ball game. The veterans seemed to know it from the minute Brad made his first call. He had something that lifted us all and made us play a little bit better than we really could play and a whole lot better than we had been playing all afternoon. He had so much confidence in us that he made us believe in ourselves completely. He made us play as well as he knew we could play. I don't know how one man can do that for a whole team, but he did it."

"I wish I had known how confident you felt," Laguerre said. "I was on the sideline, and all I could think of was that I wanted to get in the ball game. I thought we had had it, Spider. I couldn't understand why Steadman wouldn't put me in and go for a bomb. He could have had a three deep receiver spread, with me, and you, and Dick. We're all faster than most of the Cowboy secondary."

Howard looked at the youngster indulgently. He had been with the club for over four years, and although he still played second fiddle to Thomas, he was a veteran.

"That would have been the worst thing we could have done," he pointed out. "With you and Dick and Spider in a spread, the Cowboys would have taken out a linebacker, put in another defensive back, and cut off the deep pass completely. We had plenty of time to work the ball, and that's what Brad did."

"I still think we could have used more speed in the backfield," Laguerre said. "I know I'm not as good a back as Ottum, or Werner, or Tilson yet, but none of them are what you would call game breakers, Frog. They'll get yardage, but mostly they won't go all the way."

Howard shook his head and grinned.

"I guess all running backs have to be cocky," he said. "And a little nuts. No one in his right mind would spend Sunday afternoon running into 270-pound defensive tackles. Sure, you're faster than the veterans. So is Weiskopf. But you haven't spent any time under the kind of pressure they were under, Rabbit. You might have broken a long run, but you might have fumbled, too. Or blown a play or missed a block. Steadman was right."

"That's the other thing I learned," Spider put in. "I was

resentful at first when Brad went to the older guys on the drive, but then I began to understand it. They had been there before and with him. He knew what they could produce under pressure, and they knew what he could do. He couldn't afford to take a chance on any unknown quantities with the championship at stake. He told me that once before, but I didn't believe him. He made a believer out of me in Dallas."

"So where does that leave us?" Laguerre said rebelliously. "We get in when the game is over, is that it?"

"For a while, that's it," Howard said. "When you have proved yourself under fire, you can carry the load, Laguerre, old buddy."

"When do I get the chance to prove myself?" Laguerre asked. "All I do is run back kickoffs, and punts, and go down under them."

"You'll get in more and more," Frog said. "Be patient."

"He's right," Spider said. "It takes time, Rabbit. But if you've got it, you'll get a chance to prove it."

The steaks came then and interrupted the conversation. They ate in silence with the healthy appetites of young athletes, and when they had finished, Sproutt came over and sat down for a few minutes. The restaurant had filled up by now, but none of the other Rams were there, which surprised Spider a little. It was a favorite dining place for the football players not only of the Rams, but of most visiting clubs.

"Steaks all right?" Johnny asked and they nodded. "Good," he said. "Hope they feed you guys all right in Florida. Can't understand why they had to play this game down there."

210

In Florida, the steaks turned out to be very good. The Rams trained at Fort Lauderdale and stayed in a luxurious motel on the beach; the Chargers were a few miles farther north, at Boca Raton.

The routine of preparing for the Super Bowl game was not measurably different from the preparation for any league game, except that the coaches had had more time to prepare and had more practice sessions in which to inculcate the plans into the players. As always, Spider found himself admiring the care with which they had made their preparations. Their analyses of the Charger offense and defense had taken every possible contingency into consideration and worked out an answer for it.

The mood of the players was almost a relaxed one, but beneath the surface casualness, Spider could sense a strong feeling of dedication. Although he had gained a deep respect for the skills and the poise of the veterans and would have been happy to have forgotten the differences he had had during the season, he found that they were still reserved and stiff with him and with the young players as a group. In trying to analyze their feelings, he decided that they were, in effect, withholding judgment and approbation until they felt that Spider and the other young lions had done something to prove their worth.

Their attitudes differed with individuals, of course. Skeeter Tilson, the big Negro fullback, seemed to feel closer to the rookies and the second- and third-year players than the other veterans, and he was friendly with Spider.

One afternoon, sitting by the motel pool after practice, he discussed with Spider how he and the other veterans felt about the game. Spider had said that he was surprised that they seemed to take it with the same relaxed air that they took any other game.

"I try to act that way, too," he said. "But underneath, I know how much it means. Sometimes I get butterflies just thinking about dropping a ball or making a mistake. I guess it takes time to get over that."

Tilson grinned, the teeth startlingly white against his black face.

"You never get over it, Spider," he said. "If we looked relaxed, it's because we have learned to be good actors. I get butterflies, too. It's not just the money involved, although I guarantee you the fifteen gees the winning players get means a lot to me and to all of us. I don't think there are any millionaires playing on this team. But the one thing that really puts the monkey on your back, is your responsibility."

"You have that in every game," Spider said. "Maybe more in this one, but I feel it every game we play."

"Not the same way," Skeeter said. "You know you're going to lose a game every now and then in the NFL, and it's no disgrace. But in this game, I'm not just the fullback for the Los Angeles Rams, and you're not just the Ram spread end, Spider."

"What do you mean?"

"I represent all the fullbacks in the NFL," Skeeter said. "And you represent all the spread ends. And if you blow it, Spider, you're not just letting the Rams down. You're letting every spread end in the league down."

Spider thought about that for a moment and grimaced.

"I wish you hadn't told me that," he said. "I had troubles enough before."

Chapter 20

By the time the team got into the bus for the long ride to the Orange Bowl, not even the veterans could conceal the tension they felt. The ride was a quiet one, with an occasional attempt at humor by one player or another, but no one laughed. They filed into the dressing room at the Orange Bowl silently, and Spider could not remember any game since he had been with the Rams in which the club had seemed as keyed up. He did not know whether that was a good symptom or a bad one.

The hordes of sports writers who had invaded Miami for the game had speculated at length on whether or not a veteran team such as the Rams, a team which was used to winning and had, indeed, won Super Bowl games before, could possibly be mentally ready for this one. The consensus was that they could not.

Ed Pope, writing in one of the Miami papers, had summed it up.

"For the Chargers," Pope had written, "this is a crusade. For the Rams, it's just another trip to the bank."

Spider wished that Pope and the other writers could be in the dressing room to feel the tension. He doubted that the San Diego club could be any more completely prepared psychologically.

The game was only a few minutes old before he found out that the San Diego team was, indeed, embarked on a crusade. They played with an abandon and a fury that no team Spider had ever seen had matched, and each player on the club seemed to have a personal vendetta to settle with his opposite number on the Rams.

On the first pattern Spider ran, Slim Chapin, the Charger defensive back, slammed into him at the line of scrimmage. He was a big back and a quick one, but Spider knew that he did not have exceptional speed. He bounced off the contact, cut to the sideline, and Thomas hit him with a short pass. As he caught the ball, Chapin hit him on the helmet with a swinging forearm, and Spider saw stars for a moment. The play gained three yards, and as Spider got up, Chapin said, "Next time, I'll take your head off, big shot. Remember that."

Spider looked at him and laughed.

"Did you hit me?" he said. "I thought I stumbled."

The Ram attack sputtered and died out and Terrell punted; the Charger offensive unit attacked with the same passion that their defense had shown. Their quarterback was a tall, strong reject from an NFL team. His name was Johnny Mazziotta. He was a graduate of Ohio State, where he had not thrown many passes, and he went to Cleveland, an NFL club with two good quarterbacks, so that he was cut quickly.

He had been picked up by the Chargers and, after a year on their taxi squad, he had moved up when the Charger quarterback was injured. During the last four years, he had played regularly and developed quickly. Now he was the best quarterback in the AFL, and some writers considered him the best in football. He had a deep and burning desire to prove himself to the NFL which had rejected him, and his spirit infected the rest of the Charger club.

They moved with shocking ease on their first drive, and Mazziotta himself negotiated the last six yards. He rolled out to his left, faked a pass, then ran the ball over, carrying corner back Sandy Crichton over the goal line with him. On the sideline, Spider watched unbelievingly.

The Ram offense had no better luck on the next series. The rabid Charger defense kept them off balance, and the Los Angeles attack stuttered and missed; again Terrell had to come in and punt after three downs. His high, long punt set the Chargers back deep in their own territory, and this time, Mazziotta found that the Ram defense had adjusted and tightened. The Chargers moved, but they moved slowly and painfully, and the drive ended with a 37-yard field goal.

On the sideline while the Ram defense toiled, Thomas consulted with Al Berman and talked to the Ram coaches in the press box. Nothing was basically wrong with the Ram game plan; it was failing because of a breakdown in execution. The team was not playing cohesively, and Berman, talking to

Thomas near the little table which held the telephone to the press box, shook his head.

"Try them with traps and screens," he said. "They're penetrating fast, and you may be able to sting them. But nothing is going to work unless we get together and work as a team. I don't understand what has happened."

"I think I do," Brad said. Spider, sitting on the bench within earshot, looked at him hopefully, but the Ram quarterback added nothing to his comment.

Berman looked at Thomas quizzically and said, "If you know anything I don't, you better tell me now."

"It wouldn't help," Thomas said. He watched as the Chargers kicked off, and Weiskopf fielded the ball on the Ram 3-yard line and fought his way out to the 22. Thomas glanced at Spider, who was standing and putting his helmet on. "It's not a coaching problem," he said, snapping his own chin strap into place.

Because the bulk of the Ram offensive team was basically professional and blooded in big games, they improved as the half went on. The club still did not move with the overwhelming power and precision which was its trademark, but it moved well enough to keep the Chargers at bay. Thomas, under stress, depended on his veterans, and the veterans produced with professional competence, if not with brilliance. The Chargers scored once more and at the half, they led 17-0.

The dressing room was absolutely quiet after the Rams had filed in and slumped down on the benches in front of their lockers. The trainer moved among the players offering them orange halves to suck on and checking equipment, but he said nothing, and the coaches had not come out of their private room.

Steadman came out first and stood in the middle of the room, looking around at the players. His face was somber and strained, and he stood silently for a long moment.

"There will be no changes in the game plan," he said finally. "The plan works. You are behind because *you* have failed. Brad Thomas has asked us to leave the dressing room during the half, and we're leaving."

He looked at them for another long moment, then walked out with the assistant coaches following him.

The players watched them go in stunned silence. Spider looked at Thomas, and the Ram team captain stood up and walked slowly to the middle of the room.

"We are just about to make history," he said wryly. "All of us. We're just about to be the first National Football League team ever to lose a championship game to the American Football League."

He paused and searched for words.

"This is just a game," he said finally. "So I guess it's not really that important. But in a way, it's more important than any game in my life and in yours. For the rest of my life—and yours—the first thing anyone will think of when I meet them is that I was the quarterback of the Rams the year they lost to the AFL. They will wonder why I lost, and what was wrong with me, and if it is still wrong with me. I wouldn't mind if we were being beaten by a better ball club. If San Diego was kicking the hell out of us because they were so much better we couldn't do anything about it, there would be no disgrace in losing to them."

217

His face was grim and angry, and he looked slowly around the room. Spider met his eyes and looked away.

"But that's not so," Brad said. "We are a better club than the Chargers. The Cowboys were a better club than the Chargers. I've played enough pro football to know whether we are capable of beating any team, and we are capable of beating this one. They are beating us because the Chargers are a team and they are playing with complete and total dedication to the team."

He stopped again and took a deep breath.

"We're not," he said. "We haven't been for over two months. We are a group of veterans busy being proud of being veterans and some young players resenting the veterans. We are split, and divided, and selfish, and we are going to lose because of it."

He walked over to the ice cooler and picked up a paper cup of water and drank from it.

"Well," he said at last. "I was as much at fault as anyone in creating the factions. I'm sorry. Coach Steadman told me that he would respect anything we do in here, and I have tried to figure out what to do. I don't seem to be able to inspire you to play unselfishly, so I better step down. Frog, you play the second half."

There was a long moment's silence when he had finished, then some of the veterans gathered around him and began to argue with him, but he shrugged them off. Howard expostulated with him, and he patted Frog on the shoulder.

"The veterans will play all out for you," he said. "So will the rest. Maybe they'll come alive."

The coaches came back in, and Spider watched Brad approach Steadman and explain to him what he had decided.

Steadman looked shocked, but finally he nodded, just as an official put his head in the door and said, "On the field, Rams."

To his surprise, Spider found himself on his feet and calling for attention. The players had begun to move to the door, and they stopped and looked at him.

"Listen," Spider said, embarrassed. "I don't know how to say this, but I guess I didn't know how much goes into being a pro. I know I'm not one yet, and maybe I never will be. But I'm going to do my best to be one for the next two quarters. I'm sorry."

No one said anything, and Spider wasn't quite sure what he had meant by saying he was sorry. As he followed the other players back on the field, he felt a deep, cold determination to win the game if he had to break a leg to do it.

The Rams kicked off to San Diego, and the San Diego back moved out to the Charger 11-yard line before he was almost decapitated by Rabbit Laguerre, who brushed by the blocking wedge to get to him. Mazziotta, confidently surveying the Ram defense as he stood behind the center calling the countdown, dropped back for a surprise pass from deep in Charger territory and was swarmed under on the Charger 3-yard line by linebacker Mark Shawnic. The blitzing defender slammed Mazziotta to the ground just before big Tiny Ross reached him.

The Chargers punted two downs later, and Laguerre took the punt fifteen yards to the San Diego 40-yard line. The Ram offensive team took the field, and just before they knelt in the huddle, Tilson called for a time-out. He was the offensive field captain in the absence of Brad Thomas.

Howard looked at him in amazement, then, automatically, started to the sideline to talk to the coaches.

"Hold it, Frog," Skeeter said. "This isn't a strategy time-out."

The players huddled around him, and the big Negro fullback stared at them angrily.

"I didn't have a chance to say anything in the dressing room," he said. "I'm going to say it now. We're going to win this game, and if I have to whip you guys one at a time to do it, I'll do that. We're going to be a team from now on, black or white, old or young, and we're going to win for Brad Thomas and for ourselves. That's all."

Howard leaned into the huddle and called a running play, and they came out silently, without the hand clap they usually gave as they left.

At the snap of the ball, the offensive line moved in a quick, coordinated surge, and Tilson slashed through a small hole and bowled over the middle linebacker. He cut back and carried two tacklers for three yards, and the play gained six.

If the Ram fans in the stands and watching on television had expected Frog to make a dramatic change in the Ram plan of attack, they were doomed to disappointment. Howard called the same plays that Brad had called, slashing at the Charger line, trapping, screening, throwing short passes. But the Ram club was operating as a single entity now, blocking viciously and operating precisely, and the plays were going for six and seven yards at a crack. The touchdown was a quick slant-in pass to Spider, who caught it with Chapin hanging on him.

By the end of the third quarter, the Rams had tied the

220

game, and early in the fourth, on another hard, violent slashing drive, they went ahead 24-17. Tilson got that touchdown on a trap up the middle from twelve yards out, barreling through a gaping hole created by Marty Nathan's devastating block at left guard on the Chargers' massive 325-pound all-league tackle. Spider had slanted across from spread end, and he hit the Charger safety head on and stood him up in time for Skeeter to slash by him into the end zone.

On the sideline, as the Ram kickoff team took the field, Tilson gathered the offensive team around him.

"I think we've proved a point," he said. "I think we owe something to the guy who made us prove it. I think Brad ought to come back in."

Even Howard joined in the quick cheer that surprised the fans in the stands. Tilson motioned to Brad, who had been manning the phone to the press box, and Thomas joined the huddle on the sideline.

"Nice going," he said as he joined them. "Dickey says keep going. No changes. They haven't adjusted. You can't adjust to blocking and tackling."

"One change," Tilson said. "You're in, Brad. We want you back."

Thomas looked quickly at Frog Howard. Frog grinned at him and nodded.

"Your turn," he said.

The Charger offense found the Ram defense as sticky as it had been steadily during the second half, and the punt came from the San Diego 11-yard line after Tiny Ross had dropped Mazziotta for a seven-yard loss attempting to pass, and Woody Woodcock, the big defensive left end, had smeared a sweep for a three-yard loss. The other play was an incomplete pass.

The punt died on the Ram 38-yard line, and Thomas grinned as he knelt to call the signal. The Rams led by only a touchdown with nine minutes to play, and Spider expected Brad to stay with the grinding offense which had been so successful in the third quarter.

"Let's shake them up a little," Brad said. He called the play, a hitch and go to Spider, and the club came out of the huddle with renewed snap and energy.

Chapin had, during the first three quarters, moved closer and closer to Spider, since the Ram calls were almost all short patterns, sideline or look-in passes. Now he had cheated up a yard or two from a normal defensive pattern, and Spider checked his position with satisfaction.

At the snap, he drove straight at Chapin, stopped and whirled as if for a pass, then turned and accelerated. As he turned, the surprised Chapin was caught coming in, and Spider was five yards in the clear before he could recover. He caught the pass over his shoulder without breaking stride and outran the Charger secondary into the end zone, to make the score 30-17.

At the sideline, Frog shook his hand while the extra point was made and grinned at him.

"I guess I'm just too conservative," he said.

For the rest of the fourth quarter, Brad gave a virtuoso performance at quarterback. The Chargers, their lead gone and their early enthusiasm turned into sudden despair, tried to recoup with long, bad-gamble passes, three of which were intercepted.

Thomas pulled out every trick in the Ram repertoire. Once

he called an end around with Spider carrying the ball, and Spider found himself alone when he turned upfield. The play was good for sixty yards and a touchdown. A halfback option pass, with Ottum throwing the ball, accounted for a 73-yard touchdown, and by the time the game ended, the Rams had destroyed a good Charger team, 45-17.

Chapter 21

The feeling in the dressing room was not one of hysterical happiness. The room was quiet but not silent. A hum of conversation went on as the players found their lockers and began to undress, and Spider, who felt a deep sense of satisfaction and of pride, supposed that the other players were feeling the same thing.

Steadman, as usual, spoke to them briefly as soon as all of them had come in.

"I'm proud of this team," he said simply. "I can't say I had much to do with your victory today, but I'm proud of what you did. I wasn't sure you could do it."

No one else made any speeches, although Spider had half expected Brad to say something. Thomas went about un-

225

dressing methodically, talking to Tiny Ross and some of the other veterans, and paying no attention to anything but getting ready to shower.

The writers were finally let in, and Spider underwent a long grilling about the relative merits of Howard and Thomas and fended off the questioners easily. He was noncommittal when asked to compare them, although he did say that Thomas's experience and poise was invaluable in a game like this one.

He was talking to Oslen, and he saw the reporter's eyes light up.

"Howard moved the club and got the lead," he said. "Thomas came in when it was all over."

"It wasn't all over," Spider said. "And you can't say it was Howard or Thomas who won the game."

"Who was it then?" Oslen asked.

Spider looked around the room at Tiny Ross, the big veteran defensive tackle, and at Skeeter Tilson, the fullback who was in his seventh year. Hoy Yuen, the massive Hawaiian offensive tackle, was slumped in front of his locker, his 30 years showing in his tired face. The other veterans were quietly going about routine preparations for leaving, and suddenly he felt a deep affection for them. Without their strength and knowledge, the Rams would not be champions of the world.

"The veterans," he said. "The old men. The guys who put in time on this club and in this league. They are the champions."

"How about the young players?" Oslen said. "You had a great day."

"I'm trying to make the club," Spider said. Oslen looked puzzled.

"You made it three years ago," he said. "What do you mean?"

Spider looked at him thoughtfully, trying to think of how to explain what he meant, then he shook his head.

"It would take too long to tell you," he said, and Oslen walked away.

He leaned over and pulled his T-shirt over his head and stood up to find a towel and go to the shower. He felt a hand on his shoulder and turned to look into the smiling eyes of Tilson. The big back slapped him on the shoulder and pushed him toward the shower roughly.

"Welcome to the club, Spider," he said, and no one had ever said anything to Spider to make him feel as proud.

227